KELLER, A SHAPESHIFTER, has been chosen to protect a new Wild Power. When she's not a panther, Keller is a tough, no-nonsense seventeen-year-old. But she meets her match in Iliana Harman, a clueless blonde who may really be the legendary Witch Child. Will Keller get annoyed and kill Iliana before she can convince Iliana to join Circle Daybreak? And what about the dashing and romantic Galen? Keller is falling in love with him—but he's destined to be the Witch Child's soulmate.

WITCHLIGHT

THE NIGHT WORLD SERIES

• •

Night World

Daughters of Darkness

Spellbinder

Dark Angel

The Chosen

Soulmate

Huntress

Black Dawn

Witchlight

NIGHT WORLD · BOOK NINE

WITCHLIGHT

L. J. SMITH

SIMON PULSE
NEW YORK LONDON TORONTO SYDNEY NEW DELHI

This book is a work of fiction. Any references to historical events, real people, or real places are used fictitiously. Other names, characters, places, and events are products of the author's imagination, and any resemblance to actual events or places or persons, living or dead, is entirely coincidental.

SIMON PULSE

An imprint of Simon & Schuster Children's Publishing Division

1230 Avenue of the Americas, New York, New York 10020

This Simon Pulse hardcover edition August 2017

Cover designed by Regina Flath

Interior designed by Mike Rosamilia

The text of this book was set in Adobe Garamond.

Manufactured in the United States of America

2 4 6 8 10 9 7 5 3 1

Library of Congress Control Number 2016948197

ISBN 978-1-4814-9820-3 (hc)

ISBN 978-1-4814-9821-0 (eBook)

For Zachary and Anna Bokulic

CHAPTER 1

The mall was so peaceful. There was no hint of the terrible thing that was about to happen.

It looked like any other shopping mall in North Carolina on a Sunday afternoon in December. Modern. Brightly decorated. Crowded with customers who knew there were only ten shopping days until Christmas. Warm, despite the chilly gray skies outside. Safe.

Not the kind of place where a monster would appear.

Keller walked past a display of "Santa Claus Through the Ages" with all her senses alert and open. And that meant a lot of senses. The glimpses she caught of herself in darkened store windows showed a high-school-aged girl in a sleek jumpsuit, with straight black hair that fell past her hips and cool gray eyes. But she knew that anybody who watched her closely was likely to see something else—a sort of prowling grace in the way she walked and an inner glow when the gray eyes focused on anything.

Raksha Keller didn't look quite human. Which was hardly surprising, because she wasn't. She was a shapeshifter, and if people looking at her got the impression of a half-tamed panther on the loose, they were getting it exactly right.

"Okay, everybody." Keller touched the pin on her collar, then pressed a finger to the nearly invisible receiver in her ear, trying to tune out the Christmas music that filled the mall. "Report in."

"Winnie here." The voice that spoke through the receiver was light, almost lilting, but professional. "I'm over by Sears. Haven't seen anything yet. Maybe she's not here."

"Maybe," Keller said shortly into the pin—which wasn't a pin at all but an extremely expensive transmission device. "But she's supposed to love shopping, and her parents said she was headed this way. It's the best lead we've got. Keep looking."

"Nissa here." This voice was cooler and softer, emotionless. "I'm in the parking lot, driving by the Bingham Street entrance. Nothing to report—wait." A pause, then the ghostly voice came back with a new tension: "Keller, we've got trouble. A black limo just pulled up outside Brody's. They know she's here."

Keller's stomach tightened, but she kept her voice level. "You're sure it's them?"

"I'm sure. They're getting out—a couple of vampires and . . . something else. A young guy, just a boy really. Maybe a shapeshifter. I don't know for sure; he isn't like anything I've seen before." The voice was troubled, and that troubled Keller. Nissa Johnson was a vampire with a brain like the Library of Congress. Something *she* didn't recognize?

"Should I park and come help you?" Nissa asked.

"No," Keller said sharply. "Stay with the car; we're going to need it for a fast getaway. Winnie and I will take care of it. Right, Winnie?"

"Oh, right, Boss. In fact, I can take 'em all on myself; you just watch."

"*You* watch your mouth, girl." But Keller had to fight the grim smile that was tugging at her lips. Winfrith Arlin was Nissa's opposite—a witch and inclined to be emotional. Her odd sense of humor had lightened some black moments.

"Both of you stay alert," Keller said, completely serious now. "You know what's at stake."

"Right, Boss." This time, both voices were subdued.

They did know.

The world.

The girl they were looking for could save the world—or destroy it. Not that she knew that . . . yet. Her name was Iliana Harman, and she had grown up as a human child. She didn't realize that she had the blood of witches in her and that she was one of the four Wild Powers destined to fight against the time of darkness that was coming.

She's about to get quite a surprise when we tell her, Keller thought.

That was assuming that Keller's team got to her before the bad guys did. But they would. They had to. There was a reason they'd been chosen to come here, when every agent of Circle Daybreak in North America would have been glad to do this job.

They were the best. It was that simple.

They were an odd team—vampire, witch, and shape-shifter—but they were unbeatable. And Keller was only seventeen, but she already had a reputation for never losing.

And I'm not about to blow that now, she thought, "This is it, kiddies," she said. "No more talking until we ID the girl. Good luck." Their transmissions were scrambled, of course, but there was no point in taking chances. The bad guys were extremely well organized.

Doesn't matter. We'll still win, Keller thought, and she paused in her walking long enough *really* to expand her senses.

It was like stepping into a different world. They were senses that a human couldn't even imagine. Infrared. She saw body heat. Smell. Humans didn't have any sense of smell, not really. Keller could distinguish Coke from Pepsi from across a room. Touch. As a panther, Keller had exquisitely sensitive hairs all over her body, especially on her face. Even in human form, she could feel things with ten times the intensity of a real human. She could feel her way in total darkness by the air pressure on her skin.

Hearing. She could hear both higher and lower pitches

than a human, and she could pinpoint an individual cough in a crowd. Sight. She had night vision like—well, like a cat's.

Not to mention more than five hundred muscles that she could move voluntarily.

And just now, all her resources were attuned to finding one teenage girl in this swarming mall. Her eyes roved over faces; her ears pricked at the sound of every young voice; her nose sorted through thousands of smells for the one that would match the T-shirt she'd taken from Iliana's room.

Then, just as she froze, catching a whiff of something familiar, the receiver in her ear came to life.

"Keller—I spotted her! Hallmark, second floor. But they're here, too."

They'd found her first.

Keller cursed soundlessly. Aloud, she said, "Nissa, bring the car around to the west side of the mall. Winnie, don't do anything. I'm coming."

The nearest escalator was at the end of the mall. But from the map in her hand, she could see that Hallmark was directly above her on the upper level. And she couldn't waste time.

Keller gathered her legs under her and jumped.

One leap, straight up. She ignored the gasps—and a few shrieks—of the people around her as she sprang. At the top of her jump, she caught the railing that fenced off the upper-level walkway. She hung for a second by her hands, then pulled herself up smoothly.

More people were staring. Keller ignored them. They got out of her way as she headed for the Hallmark store.

Winnie was standing with her back to the display window of the store beside it. She was short, with a froth of strawberry curls and a pixie face. Keller edged up to her, careful to keep out of the line of sight of the Hallmark.

"What's up?"

"There's three of them," Winnie murmured in a barely audible voice. "Just like Nissa said. I saw them go in—and then I saw her. They've got her surrounded, but so far they're just talking to her." She glanced sideways at Keller with dancing green eyes. "Only three—we can take them easy."

"Yeah, and that's what worries me. Why would they only send three?"

Winnie shrugged slightly. "Maybe they're like us—the best."

Keller only acknowledged that with a flicker of her eyebrows. She was edging forward centimeter by centimeter, trying to get a glimpse of the interior of the Hallmark shop between the stockings and stuffed animals in the display window.

There. Two guys in dark clothing almost like uniforms—vampire thugs. Another guy Keller could see only as a partial silhouette through a rack of Christmas ornaments.

And her. Iliana. The girl everybody wanted.

She was beautiful, almost impossibly so. Keller had seen a picture, and it had been beautiful, but now she saw that it hadn't come within miles of conveying the real girl. She had the silvery-fair hair and violet eyes that showed her Harman blood. She also had an extraordinary delicacy of features and grace of movement that made her as pretty to watch as a white kitten on the grass. Although Keller knew she was seventeen, she seemed slight and childlike. Almost fairylike. And right now, she was listening with wide, trusting eyes to whatever the silhouette guy was saying.

To Keller's fury, she couldn't make it out. He must be whispering.

"It's really her," Winnie breathed from beside Keller, awed. "The Witch Child. She looks just like the legends said, just like I imagined." Her voice turned indignant. "I can't stand to watch *them* talk to her. It's like—blasphemy."

"Keep your hair on," Keller murmured, still searching with her eyes. "You witches get so emotional about your legends."

"Well, we should. She's not just a Wild Power, she's a pure soul." Winfrith's voice was softly awed. "She must be so wise, so gentle, so farsighted. I can't wait to talk to her." Her voice sharpened. "And those thugs shouldn't be *allowed* to talk to her. Come on, Keller, we can take them fast. Let's go."

"Winnie, don't—"

It was too late. Winnie was already moving, heading straight into the shop without any attempt at concealment.

Keller cursed again. But she didn't have any choice now. "Nissa, stand by. Things are going to get exciting," she snapped, touching her pin, and then she followed.

Winnie was walking directly toward the little group of three guys and Iliana as Keller reached the door. The guys were looking up, instantly alert. Keller saw their faces and gathered herself for a leap.

But it never happened. Before she could get all her muscles ready, the silhouette guy turned—and everything changed.

Time went into slow motion. Keller saw his face clearly, as if she'd had a year to study it. He wasn't bad-looking—quite handsome, actually. He didn't look much older than she was, and he had clean, nicely molded features. He had a small, compact body with what looked like hard muscles under his clothes. His hair was black, shaggy but shiny, almost like fur. It fell over his forehead in an odd way, a way that looked deliberately disarrayed and was at odds with the neatness of the rest of him.

And he had eyes of obsidian.

Totally opaque.

Shiny silver-black, with nothing clear or transparent about them. They revealed nothing; they simply threw light back at anyone who looked into them. They were the eyes of a monster, and every one of Keller's five hundred voluntary muscles froze in fear.

She didn't need to hear the roar that was far below the pitch that human ears could pick up. She didn't need to see the swirl of dark energy that flared like a red-tinged black aura around him. She knew already, instinctively, and she tried to get the breath to yell a warning to Winnie.

There was no time.

She could only watch as the boy's face turned toward Winnie and power exploded out of him.

He did it so casually. Keller could tell that it was only a flick of his mind, like a horse slapping its tail at a fly. But the dark power slammed into Winnie and sent her flying through the air, arms and legs outstretched, until she hit a wall covered with display plates and clocks. The crash was tremendous.

Winnie! Keller almost yelled it out loud.

Winnie fell behind the cash register counter, out of Keller's line of sight. Keller couldn't tell if she were alive or not. The cashier who had been standing behind the counter went running and screaming toward the back of the shop. The customers scattered, some following the cashier, some dashing for the exit.

Keller hung in the doorway a second longer as they streamed out around her. Then she reeled away to stand with her back against the window of the next shop, breathing hard. There were coils of ice in her guts.

A dragon.

He was a *dragon.*

CHAPTER 2

They'd gotten a dragon.

Keller's heart was pounding.

Somehow, somewhere, the people of the Night World had found one and awakened him. And they'd paid him—bribed him—to join their side. Keller didn't even want to imagine what the price might have been. Bile rose in her throat, and she swallowed hard.

Dragons were the oldest and most powerful of the shape-shifters, and the most evil. They had all gone to sleep thirty thousand years ago—or, rather, they had been put to sleep by the witches. Keller didn't know exactly how it had been done, but all the old legends said the world had been better off since.

And now one was back.

But he might not be fully awake yet. From the glimpse she'd had, his body was still cold, not much heat radiating from it. He'd be sluggish, not mentally alert.

It was the chance of a lifetime.

Keller's decision was made in that instant. There was no time to think about it—and no need. The inhabitants of the Night World wanted to destroy the human world. And there were plenty of them to do it, vampires and dark witches and ghouls. But *this* was something in another league altogether. With a dragon on their side, the Night World would easily crush Circle Daybreak and all other forces that wanted to save the humans from the end of the world that was coming. It would be no contest.

And as for that little girl in there, Iliana the Witch Child, the Wild Power meant to help save humankind—she would get swatted like a bug if she didn't obey the dragon.

Keller couldn't let that happen.

Even as Keller was thinking it, she was changing. It was strange to do it in a public place, in front of people. It went against all her most deeply ingrained training. But she didn't have time to dwell on that.

It felt good. It always did. Painful in a nice way, like the feeling of having a tight bandage removed. A release.

Her body was changing. For a moment, she didn't feel like anything—she almost had no body. She was fluid, a being of pure energy, with no more fixed form than a candle flame. She was utterly . . . free.

And then her shoulders were pulling in, and her arms were becoming more sinewy. Her fingers were retracting, but in their place long, curved claws were extending. Her legs were twisting, the joints changing. And from the sensitive place at the end of her spine, the place that always felt unfinished when she was in human form, something long and flexible was springing. It lashed behind her with fierce joy.

Her jumpsuit was gone. The reason was simple: she wore only clothes made out of the hair of other shapeshifters. Even her boots were made of the hide of a dead shifter. Now both were being replaced by her own fur, thick black velvet with darker black rosettes. She felt complete and whole in it.

Her arms—now her front legs—dropped to the ground, her paws hitting with a soft but heavy thump. Her face prickled with sensitivity; there were long, slender whiskers extending from her cheeks. Her tufted ears twitched alertly.

A rasping growl rose in her chest, trying to escape from her throat. She held it back—that was easy and instinctive. A panther was by nature the best stalker in the world.

The next thing she did was instinctive, too. She took a moment to gauge the distance from herself to the black-haired boy. She took a step or two forward, her shoulders low. And then she jumped.

Swift. Supple. Silent. Her body was in motion. It was a high, bounding leap designed to take a victim without an instant of warning. She landed on the dark boy's back, clinging with razor claws.

Her jaws clamped on the back of his neck. It was the way panthers killed, by biting through the spine.

The boy yelled in rage and pain, grabbing at her as her weight knocked him to the ground. It didn't do any good. Her claws were too deep in his flesh to be shaken off, and her jaws were tightening with bone-crushing pressure. A little blood spilled into her mouth, and she licked it up automatically with a rough, pointed tongue.

More yelling. She was dimly aware that the vampires were attacking her, trying to wrench her away, and that the security guards were yelling. She ignored it all. Nothing mattered but taking the life under her claws.

She heard a sudden rumble from the body beneath her. It was lower in pitch than anything human ears could pick up, but to Keller it was both soft and frighteningly loud.

Then the world exploded in agony.

The dragon had caught hold of her fur just above the right shoulder. Dark energy was crackling into her, searing her. It was the same black power he'd used against Winnie, except that now he had direct contact.

The pain was scalding, nauseating. Every nerve ending in Keller's body seemed to be on fire, and her shoulder was a solid red blaze. It made her muscles convulse involuntarily and spread a metallic taste through her mouth, but it didn't make her let go. She held on grimly, letting the waves of energy roll through her, trying to detach her mind from the pain.

What was frightening was not just the power but the sense of the dragon's mind beneath it. Keller could feel a terrible coldness. A core of mindless hatred and evil that seemed to reach back into the mists of time. This creature was old. And although Keller couldn't tell what he wanted with the present age, she knew what he was focused on right now.

Killing her. That was all he cared about.

And of course he was going to succeed. Keller had known that from the beginning.

But not before I kill you, she thought.

She had to hurry, though. There almost certainly were other Night People in the mall. These guys could call for reinforcements, and they would probably get them.

You can't . . . make me . . . let go, she thought.

She was fighting to close her jaws. He was much tougher than a normal human. Panther jaws could crush the skull of a young buffalo. And right now, she could hear muscle crunching, but still she couldn't finish him.

Hang on . . . hang on . . .

Black pain . . . blinding . . .

She was losing consciousness.

For Winnie, she thought.

Sudden strength filled her. The pain didn't matter anymore. She tossed her head, trying to break his neck, wrenching it back and forth.

The body underneath her convulsed violently. She could

feel the little lapsing in it, the weakening that meant death was close. Keller felt a surge of fierce joy.

And then she was aware of something else. Someone was pulling her off the dragon. Not in the fumbling way the thugs had. This person was doing it skillfully, touching pressure points to make her claws retract, even getting a finger into her mouth, under the short front teeth between the lethal canines.

No! Keller thought. From her panther throat came a short, choking snarl. She lashed out with her back legs, trying to rip the person's guts out.

No. The voice didn't come in through Keller's ears. It was in her mind. A boy's voice. And it wasn't afraid, despite the fact that she was now scrabbling weakly, still trying to turn his stomach to spaghetti. It was concerned and anxious but not afraid. *Please—you have to let go.*

Even as he said it, he was pushing more pressure points. Keller was already weak. Now, all at once, she saw stars. She felt her hold on the dragon loosen.

And then she was being jerked backward, and she was falling. A hundred and ten pounds of black panther was landing on whoever had yanked her free.

Dizzy . . .

Her vision was blurred, and her body felt like rubber. She hardly had enough strength to twist her head toward the boy who had pulled her away.

Who was he? *Who?*

Her eyes met blazing green-gold ones.

Almost the eyes of a leopard. It gave Keller a jolt. But the rest of the boy was different. Dark gold hair over a rather pale and strained face with perfectly sculpted features. Human, of course. And those eyes seemed to be blazing with worry and intensity rather than animal ferocity.

Not many people could look at an angry panther like that.

She heard his mental voice again. *Are you all right?*

And then, for just an instant, something happened. It was as if some barrier had been punctured. Keller felt not just his voice but his *worry* inside her head. She could feel . . . him.

His name . . . Galen. And he's someone born to command, she thought. He understands animals. Another shapeshifter?

But I can't feel what animal he turns into. And there's no bloodthirstiness at all. . . .

She didn't understand it, and her panther brain wasn't in the mood to try. It was grounded in the here and now, and all it wanted was to finish what she had started.

She wrenched her eyes away from Galen and looked at the dragon.

Yes, he was still alive but badly wounded. A little snarl worked out of Keller's throat. The vampire thugs were still alive, too; one was picking up the injured dragon and hauling him away.

"Come on!" he was shouting in a voice sharp with panic. "Before that cat recovers—"

"But the girl!" the second vampire said. "We don't have the girl." He looked around. Iliana was standing by a display of porcelain figures, looking just as pale and graceful as any of them. She had both hands at her throat and seemed to be in shock.

The second vampire started toward her.

No, Keller thought. But she couldn't get her legs to move. She could only lie helplessly and stare with burning eyes.

"No!" a voice beside her said, out loud this time. Galen was jumping up. He got between the vampire and Iliana.

The vampire grinned, a particularly nasty grin. "You don't look like a fighter to me, pretty boy."

It wasn't exactly true, Keller thought. Galen wasn't pretty; he was beautiful. With that gold hair and his coloring, he looked like a prince from a storybook. A rather young and inexperienced prince. He stood his ground, his expression grim and determined.

"I won't let you get to her," he said steadily.

Who the hell is this guy? Keller thought.

Iliana, pale and wide-eyed, glanced up at him, too. And then Keller saw her . . . melt. Her drawn features softened; her lips parted. Her eyes seemed to quiver with light. She had been cowering away from the vampire, but now her body relaxed just a little.

He certainly *looked* more like a champion defender than Keller had. He was clean, for one thing. Keller's fur was matted with her own blood and the dragon's. More, she couldn't help the little raspy snarls of rage and despair she was making, showing dripping teeth in a red-stained muzzle.

Too bad he was about to be slaughtered.

He *wasn't* a fighter. Keller had seen the inside of his mind, and she knew he didn't have the tiger instinct. The vampire was going to massacre him.

The vampire started forward.

And a voice from the front of the store said, "Hold it right there."

CHAPTER 3

Keller turned her head quickly.

Nissa was standing there, cool and imperturbable as always, one hand on her hip. Her short mink-colored hair wasn't even ruffled; her eyes, just a shade or two darker, were steady. And she was holding an ironwood fighting stick with a very sharp point.

Keller growled faintly in relief. You couldn't ask Nissa to be creative—her mind didn't work that way. But on any question of logic, she was unbeatable, and she had nerves of ice. More important right now, she was a superb fighter.

"If you want to play, why don't you try me?" she suggested, and whipped the fighting stick around expertly a few times. It whistled in the air, traced a complicated figure, and ended up casually across her shoulder. Then she slowly extended the point toward the vampire's throat.

"Yeah, and don't leave me out." This voice was husky and

shaky but still grim. It came from behind the counter. Winnie was pulling herself up. She coughed once, then stood straight, facing the vampire. Energy, orange and pulsating, flared between her cupped hands. Witch power.

You're alive, Keller thought. She couldn't suppress the flash of relief.

The vampire looked from one girl to the other. Then he glanced at Keller, who was lying on her side, feebly trying to make her legs work. Her tail lashed furiously.

"Come *on*!" the other vampire shouted. He was staggering under the weight of the dragon, heading for the door. "Let's get Azhdeha out of here. He's the most important thing."

The first vampire hesitated one instant, then whirled and plunged after his friend. Together, they hustled the dragon out into the mall.

Then they were gone.

Keller gave one final gasping snarl and felt herself change. This time, it felt more like a snail falling out of a shell. Her claws dissolved, her tail withered, and she slumped into her human body.

"Boss! Are you okay?" Winnie came toward her, a little unsteadily.

Keller raised her head, black hair falling on either side to the floor. She pushed herself up with her arms and looked around, taking stock.

The shop was quiet. It was also a wreck. Winnie's impact

with the wall had knocked off most of the decorative plates and clocks there. Keller's fight with the dragon had trashed a lot of the shelves. There were shattered Christmas ornaments everywhere, little glittering fragments of scarlet and holly green and royal purple. It was like being in a giant kaleidoscope.

And outside, chaos was gathering. The entire fight had only taken about five minutes, but all the time it had been going on, people had been running away from the shop and screaming. Keller had noticed them; she had simply filed them away in her mind as unimportant. There had been nothing she could do about them.

Now, there were security officers closing in, and someone had undoubtedly called the police.

She pushed with her arms again and managed to stand up.

"Nissa." It hurt her throat to speak. "Where's the car?"

"Right down *there.*" Nissa pointed at the floor. "Directly below us, parked outside the Mrs. Fields cookie store."

"Okay. Let's get Iliana out." Keller looked at the young girl with the shimmering hair who as yet hadn't spoken a single word. "Can you walk?"

Iliana stared at her. She didn't say anything. Stunned and frightened, Keller guessed. Well, a lot had happened in the last few minutes.

"I know this all seems bizarre to you, and you're probably wondering who we are. I'll explain everything. But right now, *we have to get out of here.* Okay?"

Iliana shrank a little, trembling.

Not exactly a hero, Keller thought. *Or* quick on the uptake. Then she decided she was being unfair. This girl was the Witch Child; she undoubtedly had hidden strengths.

"Come on," Galen said to Iliana gently. "She's right; it isn't safe here."

Iliana looked up at him earnestly. She seemed about to agree. Then she gave a little shiver, shut her eyes, and fainted.

Galen caught her as she fell.

Keller stared.

"She's too pure to deal with this kind of stuff," Winnie said defensively. "Violence and all. It's not the same as being *chicken.*"

It was at that exact moment that Keller could pinpoint her first real doubts about the new Wild Power.

Galen looked down at the girl who lay in his arms like a broken lily. He looked at Keller.

"I—"

"You take her; we'll surround you and cover you," Keller said, cutting him off. She knew her hair was in complete disarray, a wild cyclone of black around her. Her sleek jumpsuit was torn and stained, and she was clutching her right shoulder, which still throbbed in agony. But she must have looked fairly commanding, because Galen didn't say another word, just nodded and started toward the door.

Nissa led the way in front of him. Winnie and Keller fell

in behind. They were ready to fight, but when the security guards with walkie-talkies saw Nissa whirling her stick, they backed away. The ordinary people, curious onlookers attracted by all the noise, not only backed away but ran. Lots of them screamed.

"Go," Keller said. "Fast. Go."

They made it to Mrs. Fields without anybody trying to stop them.

A girl with a red apron flattened herself against a wall as they thrust their way behind the counter and into the sanctum full of industrial-sized ovens in the back. A gangly boy dropped a tray with a clang, and lumps of raw cookie dough scattered on the floor.

And then they were bursting through the back entrance, and there was the car, a white limousine illegally parked at the curb. Nissa whipped out a key chain and pressed a button, and Keller heard the click of doors unlocking.

"Inside!" she said to Galen. He got in. Winnie ran around the car to get in the other side. Nissa slid into the driver's seat. Keller ducked in last and snapped, "Go!" even as she slammed the door.

Nissa floored it.

The limousine shot forward like a dolphin—just as a security truck sped up from the rear. A police car appeared dead in front of them.

Nissa was an excellent driver. The limo swerved with a

squeal of tires and peeled out of another of the parking lot's exits. A second police car swung toward them as Nissa dodged traffic. This one had lights and sirens on. Nissa gunned the engine, and the limo surged forward again. A freeway on-ramp was ahead.

"Hang on," Nissa said briefly.

They were passing the on-ramp—they were past it. No, they weren't. At the last possible second, the limo screamed into a ninety-degree turn. Everyone inside was thrown around. Keller clenched her teeth as her wounded arm hit the window. Then they were shooting up the on-ramp and onto the freeway.

With a little patter, cat's paws of rain appeared on the windshield. Keller, leaning forward to look over Nissa's shoulder, was happy. With icy rain and the low, gray fog, they probably wouldn't be chased by helicopter. The big limousine roared past the few other cars on the road, and Winnie sat looking out the rear window, murmuring a spell to confuse and delay any pursuit.

"We lost them," Nissa said. Keller sat back and let out her breath. For the first time since she'd entered the mall, she allowed herself to relax minutely.

We did it.

At the same moment, Winnie turned. She pounded the backseat with a small, hard fist. "We did it! Keller—we got the Wild Power! We . . ." Her voice trailed off as she saw Keller's face. "And, uh . . . I guess I disobeyed orders." Her pounding was self-conscious now; she ducked her strawberry blond head. "Um, I'm sorry, Boss."

"You'd better be," Keller said. She held Winnie's gaze a moment, then said, "You could have gotten yourself killed, witch—and for absolutely no good reason."

Winnie grimaced. "I know. I lost it. I'm sorry." But she smiled timidly at Keller afterward. Keller's team knew how to read her.

"Sorry, too, Boss," Nissa said from the front seat. She slanted a glance at Keller from her mink-colored eyes. "I wasn't supposed to leave the car."

"But you thought we might need a little help," Keller said. She nodded, meeting Nissa's eyes in the mirror. "I'm glad you did."

The faintest flush of pleasure colored Nissa's cheeks.

Galen cleared his throat.

"Um, for the record, I'm sorry, too. I didn't mean to charge in like that in the middle of your operation."

Keller looked at him.

He was smiling slightly, hesitantly, the way Winnie had. A nice smile. The corner of his mouth naturally quirked upward, giving him a hint of mischief in all but the most serious moments. His green-gold eyes were apologetic but hopeful.

"Yeah, who are you, guy?" Winnie was looking him up and down, her dark lashes twinkling. "Did Circle Daybreak send you? I thought we were on this mission alone."

"You were. I belong to Circle Daybreak, but they didn't send me. I just—well, I was outside the shop, and I couldn't just stand there . . ." His voice died. The smile died, too. "You're really mad, aren't you?" he said to Keller.

"Mad?" She took a slow breath. *"I'm furious."*

He blinked. "I don't—"

"You stopped me, I could have killed him!"

His gold-green eyes opened in shock and something like remembered pain. "He was killing *you.*"

"I know that," Keller snarled. "It doesn't matter what happens to me. What matters is that now he's free. Don't you understand what he is?"

Winfrith was looking sober. "*I* don't know. But he hit me with something powerful. Pure energy like what I use, but about a hundred times stronger."

"He's a dragon," Keller said. She saw Nissa's shoulders stiffen, but Winnie just shook her head, bewildered. "A kind of shapeshifter that hasn't been around for about thirty thousand years."

"He can turn into a *dragon*?"

Keller didn't smile. "No, of course not. Don't be silly. I don't know what he can do—but a dragon is what he *is*. Inside." Winnie suddenly looked queasy as this hit home. Keller turned back to Galen.

"And that's what you let loose on the world. It was the only chance to kill him—nobody will be able to take him by surprise like that again. Which means that everything he does after this is going to be your fault."

Galen shut his eyes, looking dizzy. "I'm sorry. But when I saw you—I couldn't let you die. . . ."

"I'm expendable. I don't know who you are, but I'm willing to bet *you're* expendable. The only one here who *isn't* expendable is her." Keller jerked a thumb at Iliana, who lay in a pool of pale silver-gold hair on the seat beside Galen. "And if you think that dragon isn't going to come back and try to get her again, you're crazy. I'd have died happy knowing that I'd gotten rid of him."

Galen's eyes were open again, and Keller saw a flicker in them at the "don't know who you are." But at the end, he said quietly, "I'm expendable. And I'm sorry. I didn't think—"

"That's right! You didn't! And now the whole world is going to suffer."

Galen shut up and sat back.

And Keller felt odd. She wasn't sorry for slapping him down, she told herself. He deserved it.

But his face was so pale now, and his expression was so bleak. As if he'd not only understood everything she'd said but expanded on it in his own mind. And the look of hurt in his eyes was almost insupportable.

Good, Keller told herself. But then she remembered the moment she'd spent inside his mind. It had been a sunlit place, warm and open, without dark corners or shadowed crevasses.

Now that would be gone forever. There was going to be a huge black fissure in it, full of horror and shame. A mark he would carry for the rest of his life.

Well, welcome to the real world, Keller thought, and her throat tightened and hurt. She stared out the window angrily.

"See, it's really important that we keep Iliana safe," Winfrith was saying quietly to Galen. He didn't ask why, and Keller had noticed before that he hadn't asked why Iliana wasn't expendable. But Winnie went on telling him anyway. "She's a Wild Power. You know about those?"

"Who doesn't these days?" He said it almost in a whisper.

"Well, most *humans*, for one thing. But she's not just a Wild Power; she's the Witch Child. Somebody we witches have been expecting for centuries. The prophecies say she's going to unite the shapeshifters and the witches. She's going to marry the son of the First House of the shapeshifters. And then the two races will be united, and all the shapeshifters will join Circle Daybreak, and we'll be able to hold off the end of the world at the millennium." Winnie finished out of breath. Then she cocked her strawberry blond head. "You don't seem surprised. Who *are* you, guy? You didn't really say before."

"Me?" He was still looking into the distance. "I'm nobody, compared to you people." Then he gave a little wry smile that didn't reach his eyes. "I'm expendable."

Nissa caught Keller's eye in the rearview mirror, looking concerned. Keller just shrugged. Sure, Winnie was telling this expendable guy a lot. But it didn't matter. He wasn't on the enemy side; anyway, the enemy knew everything Winnie was saying. They had identified Iliana as the third Wild Power; the dragon proved that. They wouldn't have sent him if they hadn't been sure.

But still, it was time to get rid of this interfering boy. They certainly couldn't take him to the safe house where they were taking Iliana.

"Nobody tailing us?" Keller said.

Nissa shook her head. "We lost them all miles ago."

"You're sure?"

"Dead certain."

"Okay. Take any exit, and we'll drop him off." She turned to Galen. "I hope you can find your way home."

"I want to go with you."

"Sorry. We have important things to do." Keller didn't need to add, *And you're not part of them.*

"Look." Galen took a deep breath. His pale face was strained and exhausted, as if he'd somehow lost three days' sleep since he'd gotten into the limo. And there was something close to desperation in his eyes. "I need to go with you. I need to help, to try and make up for what I did. I need to make it *right.*"

"You can't." Keller said it even more brusquely than she meant to. "You're not trained, and you're not involved in this. You're no good."

He gave her a look. It didn't disagree with anything she'd said, but somehow, for just an instant, it made her feel small. His greeny-gold eyes were just the opposite of the dragon's opaque ones. Keller could see for miles in them, endless light-filled fathoms, and it was all despair. A sorrow so great that it shook her.

She knew it must be costing him a lot to show her that, to hold himself so open and vulnerable. But he kept looking at her steadily.

"You don't understand," he said quietly. "I *have* to help you. I have to try, at least. I know I'm not in your class as a fighter. But I . . ." He hesitated. "I didn't want to say this—"

At that moment, Iliana groaned and sat up.

Or tried to. She didn't make it all the way. She put a hand to her head and started to fall off the seat.

Galen steadied her, putting an arm around her to keep her propped up.

"Are you all right?" Keller asked. She leaned forward, trying to get a look at the girl's face. Winnie was leaning forward, too, her expression eager.

"How're you feeling? You're not really hurt, are you? You just fainted from the shock."

Iliana looked around the limousine. She seemed utterly confused and disoriented.

Keller was struck again by the girl's unearthly beauty. This close, she looked like a flower, or maybe a girl made from flowers. She had peach-blossom skin and hazy iris-colored eyes. Her hair was like corn silk, fine and shimmering even in this dim light. Her hands were small and graceful, fingers half curled like flower petals.

"It's such an honor to meet you," Winnie said, and her voice turned formal as she uttered the traditional greeting of the witches. "Unity, Daughter of Hellewise. I'm Winfrith Arlin." She dimpled. "But it's really 'Arm-of-Lightning.' My family's an old one, almost as old as yours."

Iliana stared at her. Then she stared at the back of Nissa's mink-colored head. Then her eyes slid to Keller.

Then she sucked in a deep breath and started screaming.

CHAPTER 4

Winnie's jaw dropped.

"You—you—*keep away from me*!" Iliana said, and then she got another breath and started shrieking again. She had good lungs, Keller thought. The shrieks were not only loud, they were piercing and pitched high enough to shatter glass. Keller's sensitive ear-drums felt as if somebody were driving ice picks through them.

"All of you!" Iliana said. She was holding out both hands to fend them off. "Just let me go! I want to go home!"

Winnie's face cleared a little. "Yeah, I'll bet you do. But, you see, that place is dangerous. We're going to take you some-where safe—"

"You kidnapped me! Oh, God, I've been *kidnapped.* My parents aren't rich. What do you *want*?"

Winnie looked at Keller for help.

Keller was watching their prize Wild Power grimly. She was getting a bad feeling about this girl.

"It's nothing like that." She kept her voice quiet and level, trying to cut through the hysteria.

"You—don't you even talk to me!" Iliana waved a hand at Keller desperately. "I *saw.* You changed. You were a monster! There was blood all over—you *killed* that man." She buried her face in her hands and began to sob.

"No, she didn't." Winnie tried to put a hand on the girl's shoulder. "And anyway, he attacked me first."

"He did not. He didn't touch you." The words were muffled and jerky.

"He didn't *touch* me, no, but—" Winnie broke off, looking puzzled. She tried again. "Not with his *hands*, but—"

In the front seat, Nissa shook her head slightly, amused. "Boss—"

"I'm way ahead of you," Keller said grimly. This was going to be difficult. Iliana didn't even know that the dragon was the bad guy. All she had seen was a boy trying to talk with her, a girl inexplicably flying against a wall, and a panther that attacked unprovoked.

Keller's head hurt.

"I want to go *home*," Iliana repeated. All at once, with surprising speed, she lunged for the door handle. It took Keller's animal reflexes to block her, and the movement sent another pang through her injured shoulder.

Strangely, as it happened, pain seemed to flicker across Galen's face. He reached out and gently pulled Iliana back.

"Please don't," he said. "I know this is all really strange, but you've got it backwards. That guy who was talking to you—*he* was going to kill you. And Keller saved you. Now they want to take you somewhere safe and explain everything."

Iliana raised her head and looked at him. She looked for a long time. Finally, she said, still almost whispering, "You're all right. I can tell."

Can she? Keller wondered. Does she see something in his eyes? Or does she just see that he's a handsome blond guy with long lashes?

"So you'll go with her?" Galen asked.

Iliana gulped, sniffed, and finally nodded. "Only if you go, too. And only for a little while. After that, I want to go home."

Winfrith's face cleared—at least slightly. Keller stopped guarding the door, but she wasn't happy.

"Straight to the safe house, Boss?" Nissa asked, swinging the car back toward the freeway.

Keller nodded grimly. She glanced at Galen. "You win." She didn't have to say the rest. The girl would only go if he went. Which made him a member of the team.

For the present.

He smiled, very faintly. There was nothing smug in it, but Keller looked again.

Nothing was going the way she'd planned. And Winnie might still have faith in her Witch Child, but Keller's doubts had crystallized.

We are all, she thought, in very big trouble.

And there was a dragon that might start looking for them at any minute. How fast did dragons recover, anyway?

Big trouble, Keller thought.

The safe house was a nondescript brick bungalow. Circle Daybreak owned it, and nobody in the Night World knew about it.

That was the theory, anyway. The truth was that no place was safe. As soon as they had hidden the limo in an ivy-covered carport in back and Keller had made a phone call to Circle Daybreak headquarters, she told Winnie to set up wards around the house.

"They won't be all that strong," Winnie said. "But they'll warn us if something tries to get in." She bustled around, doing witch things to the doors and windows.

Nissa stopped Keller on her own trip of inspection. "We'd better look at your arm."

"It's all right."

"You can barely move it."

"I'll manage. Go look at Winnie; she hit that wall pretty hard."

"Winnie's okay; I already checked her. And, Keller, just because you're the team leader doesn't mean you have to be invulnerable. It's all right to accept help sometimes."

"We don't have time to waste on *me*!" Keller went back to the living room.

She'd left Iliana in the care of Galen. She hadn't actually *told* him that, but she'd left them alone together, and now she found he'd gotten a root beer from the refrigerator and some tissues from the bathroom. Iliana was sitting huddled on the couch, holding the drink and blotting her eyes. She jumped at every noise.

"Okay, now I'm going to try to explain," Keller said, pulling up an ottoman. Winnie and Nissa quietly took seats behind her. "I guess the first thing I should tell you about is the Night World. You don't know what that is, do you?"

Iliana shook her head.

"Most humans don't. It's an organization, the biggest underground organization in the world. It's made up of vampires and shapeshifters and witches—well, not witches now. Only a few of the darkest witches from Circle Midnight are still part of it. The rest of them have seceded."

"Vampires . . . ," Iliana whispered.

"Like Nissa," Keller said. Nissa smiled, a rare full smile that showed sharp teeth. "And Winnie is a witch. And you saw what I am. But we're all part of Circle Daybreak, which is an organization for everybody who wants to try to live together in peace."

"Most of the Night People hate humans," Winnie said. "Their only laws are that you can't tell humans about the Night World and that you can't fall in love with them."

"But even humans can join Circle Daybreak," Keller said.

"And that's why you want me?" Iliana looked bewildered.

"Well, not exactly." Keller ran a hand over her forehead. "Look, the main thing you need to know about Circle Daybreak is what it's trying to do right now. What it's trying to keep from happening." Keller paused, but there was no easy way to say it. "The end of the world."

"The end of the *world*?"

Keller didn't smile, didn't blink, just waited it out while Iliana sputtered, gasped, and looked at Galen for some kind of sanity. When she finally ran down, Keller went on.

"The millennium is coming. When it gets here, a time of darkness is going to begin. The vampires *want* it to happen; they want the darkness to wipe out the human race. They figure that then they'll be in charge."

"The end of the world," Iliana said.

"Yes. I can show you the evidence if you want. There are all sorts of things happening right now that prove it. The world is falling into disorder, and pretty soon it's going to fall apart. But the reason we need you is because of the prophecies."

"I want to go home."

I bet you do, Keller thought. For a moment, she felt complete sympathy for the girl. "Like this." She quoted:

"Four to stand between the light and the shadow,
Four of blue fire, power in their blood.
Born in the year of the blind Maiden's vision;
Four less one and darkness triumphs."

"I really don't know what you're *talking about*—"

"Four Wild Powers," Keller went on relentlessly. "Four people with a special gift, something nobody else has. Each one of them born seventeen years ago. If Circle Daybreak can get all four of them to work together—and *only* if Circle Daybreak can get them to work together—then we can hold off the darkness."

Iliana was shaking her head, edging away even from Galen. Behind Keller, Winnie and Nissa stood up, closing in. They faced her in a solid block, unified.

"I'm sorry," Keller said. "You can't escape it. You're part of it. You're a Wild Power."

"And you should be happy," Winnie burst out, unable to contain herself any longer. "You're going to help save the world. You know that thing I did back in the Hallmark shop? With the orange fire?" She cupped her hands. "Well, you're full of *blue* fire. And that's so much stronger—nobody even knows what it can do."

Iliana put out her hands. "I'm sorry. I *really* am. But you guys are nuts, and you've got the wrong person. I mean, I don't know, maybe you're not completely nuts. The things that happened back at that store . . ." She stopped and gulped. "But I don't have anything to do with it." She shut her eyes, as if that would bring the real world into focus. "I'm not any Wild Power," she said more firmly. "I'm just a human kid—"

"Actually, no," Nissa said.

"You're a lost witch," Winnie cut in. "You're a *Harman.* A Hearth-Woman. That's the most famous family of witches; they're like—they're royalty. And you're the most famous of all of them. You're the Witch Child. We've been waiting for you."

Keller shifted. "Winnie, maybe we don't need to tell her all of this right now."

But Winnie was racing on. "You're the one who's going to unite the shapeshifters and the witches. You're going to marry a prince of the shapeshifters, and then we're all going to be like this." She held up two intertwined fingers.

Iliana stared at her. "I'm only seventeen. I'm not marrying *anybody.*"

"Well, you can do a promise ceremony; that's binding. The witches would accept it, and I think the shapeshifters would." She glanced at Keller for confirmation.

Keller pinched the bridge of her nose. "I'm just a grunt; I can't speak for the 'shifters."

Winnie was already turning back to Iliana, her curls shaking with earnestness. "Really, you know," she said, "it's incredibly important. Right now, the Night World is split. Vampires on one side, witches on the other. And the shapeshifters—well, they could go either way. And *that's* what could determine the battle."

"Look—"

"The witches and the shapeshifters haven't been allies for thirty thousand—"

"I don't care!"

Full-blown hysteria.

It was about as scary as a six-week-old kitten hissing, but it was the best raving Iliana could manage. Both her small fists were clenched, and her face and throat were flushed.

"I don't care about the shapeshifters *or* the witches. I'm just a normal kid with a normal life, and I want to go *home*! I don't know anything about fighting. Even if I believed all this stuff, I couldn't help you. I hate PE; I'm totally uncoordinated. I get sick when I see blood. And—" She looked around and made an inarticulate sound of exasperation. "And *I lost my purse.*"

Keller stood up. "Forget your purse."

"It had my mom's credit card in it. She's going to *kill me* if I come home without that. I just—where's my purse?"

"Look, you little idiot," Keller said. "Worry about your mother, not about her credit card."

Iliana backed up a step. Even in the middle of a hysterical

fit, she was beautiful beyond words. Strands of angel-fine hair stuck to her flushed, wet cheeks. Her eyes were dark as twilight, shadowed by heavy lashes—and they wouldn't quite meet Keller's.

"I don't know what you mean."

"Yes, you do. Where's your mom going to be when the end of the world comes? Is a credit card going to save her then?"

Iliana was in a corner now. Keller could hear both Nissa and Winnie making warning noises. She knew herself that this was the wrong way to get someone on their side. But patience wasn't one of Keller's great virtues. Neither was keeping her temper.

"Let's see," Galen said, and his voice was like cool water flowing through the room. "Maybe we could take a little break—"

"I don't need advice from you," Keller snapped. "And if this little idiot is too stupid to understand that she can't turn her back on this, we have to show her."

"I'm not an idiot!"

"Then you're just a big baby? Scared?"

Iliana sputtered again. But there was unexpected fire in her violet eyes as she did it. She was looking right at Keller now, and for a moment Keller thought that there might be a breakthrough.

Then she heard a noise.

Her ears picked it up before either Winnie's or Nissa's. A car on the street outside.

"Company," Keller said. She noticed that Galen had stiffened. Had he heard it?

Winnie was moving to stand behind the door; Nissa slipped as quietly as a shadow to the window. It was dark outside now, and vampire eyes were good at night.

"Blue car," Nissa said softly. "Looks like them inside."

"Who?" Iliana said.

Keller gestured at her to be quiet. "Winnie?"

"I have to wait until they cross the wards." A pause, then she broke into a smile. "It's her!"

"Who?" Iliana said. "I thought nobody was supposed to know we were here."

Good thinking. Logical, Keller thought. "This is someone I called. Someone who came all the way from Nevada and has been waiting to see you." She went to the door.

It took a few minutes for the people in the car to get out—they moved slowly. Keller could hear the crunch of footsteps and the sound of a cane. She opened the door.

There was no light outside; the figures approaching were in shadow until they actually reached the threshold.

The woman who stepped in was old. So old that anyone's first thought on first seeing her was *How can she still be alive?* Her skin was creased into what seemed like hundreds of translucent folds. Her hair was pure white and almost as fine as Iliana's, but there wasn't much of it. Her already tiny figure was stooped almost double. She walked with a cane in one hand and the other tucked into the arm of a nondescript young man.

But the eyes that met Keller's were anything but senile. They were bright and almost steely, gray with just the faintest touch of lavender.

"The Goddess's bright blessings on you all," she said, and smiled around the room.

It was Winnie who answered. "We're honored by your presence—Grandma Harman."

In the background, Iliana demanded plaintively for the third time, "Who?"

"She's your great-great-aunt," Winnie said, her voice quiet with awe. "And the oldest of the Harmans. She's the Crone of all the Witches."

Iliana muttered something that might have been, "She looks like it."

Keller stepped in before Winnie could attack her. She introduced everyone. Grandma Harman's keen eyes flickered when Galen's turn came, but she merely nodded.

"This is my apprentice and driver, Toby," she told them. "He goes everywhere with me, so you can speak freely in front of him."

Toby helped her to the couch, and everyone else sat, too—except Iliana, who stubbornly stayed in her corner.

"How much have you told her?" Grandma Harman asked.

"Almost everything," Keller said.

"And?"

"She—isn't quite certain."

"I *am* certain," Iliana piped up. "I want to go home."

Grandma Harman extended a knobby hand toward her. "Come here, child. I want to take a look at my great-great-niece."

"I'm not your great-great-niece," Iliana said. But with those steely-but-soft eyes fixed on her, she took one step forward.

"Of course you are; you just don't know it. Do you realize, you're the image of my mother when she was your age? And I'll bet your great-grandmother looked like her, too." Grandma Harman patted the couch beside her. "Come here. I'm not going to hurt you. My name is Edgith, and your great-grandmother was my little sister, Elspeth."

Iliana blinked slowly. "Great-Grandmother Elspeth?"

"It was almost ninety years ago that I last saw her. It was just before the First World War. She and our baby brother, Emmeth, were separated from the rest of the family. We all thought they were dead, but they were being raised in England. They grew up and had children there, and eventually some of those children came to America. Without ever suspecting their real heritage, of course. It's taken us a long time to track down their descendants."

Iliana had taken another involuntary step. She seemed

fascinated by what the old woman was saying. "Mom always talked about Great-Grandmother Elspeth. She was supposed to be so beautiful that a prince fell in love with her."

"Beauty has always run in our family," Grandma Harman said carelessly. "Beauty beyond comparison, ever since the days of Hellewise Hearth-Woman, our foremother. But that isn't the important thing about being a Harman."

"It isn't?" Iliana said doubtfully.

"No." The old woman banged her cane. "The important thing, child, is the art. Witchcraft. You are a witch, Iliana; it's in your blood. It always will be. And you're the gift of the Harmans in this last fight. Now, listen carefully." Staring at the far wall, she recited slowly and deliberately:

> "One from the land of kings long forgotten;
> One from the hearth which still holds the spark;
> One from the Day World where two eyes are
> watching;
> One from the twilight to be one with the dark."

Even when she had finished, the words seemed to hang in the air of the room. No one spoke.

Iliana's eyes had changed. She seemed to be looking inside herself, at something only she could see. It was as if deeply buried memories were stirring.

"That's right," Grandma Harman said softly. "You can feel the truth of what I'm telling you. It's all there, the instinct, the art, if you just let it come out. Even the courage is there."

Suddenly, the old woman's voice was ringing. "You're the spark in the poem, Iliana. The hope of the witches. Now, what do you say? Are you going to help us beat the darkness or not?"

CHAPTER 5

Everything hung in the balance, and for a moment Keller thought that they had won. Iliana's face looked different, older and more clearly defined. For all her flower-petal prettiness, she had a strong little chin.

But she didn't say anything, and her eyes were still hazy.

"Toby," Grandma Harman said abruptly. "Put in the video."

Her apprentice went to the VCR. Keller stared at the tape in his hand, her heart picking up speed.

A video. Could that be what she thought it was?

"What you're about to see is—well, let's just say it's very secret," Grandma Harman said to Iliana as the apprentice fiddled with the controls. "So secret that there's only one tape of it, and that stays locked up in Circle Daybreak headquarters at all times. I'm the only person I trust to carry it around. All right, Toby, play it."

Iliana looked at the TV apprehensively. "What is it?"

The old woman smiled at her. "Something the enemy would really like to see. It's a record of the other Wild Powers—in action."

The first scene on the tape was live news coverage of a fire. A little girl was trapped in a second-story apartment, and the flames were getting closer and closer. Suddenly, the tape went into slow motion, and a blue flash lit the screen. When the flash died away, the fire was out.

"The blue fire," Grandma Harman said. "The first Wild Power we found did that, smothered those ordinary flames with a single thought. That's just one example of what it can do."

The next scene was of a dark-haired young man. This one was obviously deliberately filmed; the boy was looking directly into the camera. He took a knife from his belt and very coolly made a cut on his left wrist. Blood welled up in the wound and dripped to the ground.

"The second Wild Power," Grandma Harman said. "A vampire prince."

The boy turned and held out the arm that was bleeding. The camera focused on a large boulder about thirty feet away. And then the tape went into slow motion again, and Keller could actually *see* the blue fire shoot out from his hand.

It started as a burst, but what followed was a steady stream. It was so bright that the camera couldn't deal with it; it bleached out the rest of the picture. But when it hit the rock, there was no doubt about what happened.

The two-ton boulder exploded into gravel.

When the dust settled, there was only a charred crater in the ground. The dark-haired boy looked back at the camera, then shrugged and targeted another boulder. He wasn't even sweating.

Keller's breath came out involuntarily. Her heart was pounding, and she knew her eyes were glittering. She saw Galen glance sideways at her but ignored him.

Power like *that*, she thought. I never really imagined it. If I had that power, the things I could do with it . . .

Before she could help herself, she had turned to Iliana.

"Don't you see? That's what you'll bring to our side if you choose to fight with us. That's what's going to give us a *chance* against them. You have to do it, don't you understand?"

It was the wrong thing to say. Iliana's reaction to the video had been completely different from Keller's own. She was staring at the TV as if she were watching open-heart surgery. *Unsuccessful* open-heart surgery.

"I don't . . . I can't do anything like that!"

"Iliana—"

"And I don't want to! No. Look." A veil seemed to have dropped down behind Iliana's beautiful eyes. She was facing Keller, but Keller wondered if she actually saw anything. She spoke rapidly, almost frantically.

"You said you had to talk to me, so I listened. I even watched your—your special effects stuff." She waved a hand at the screen where the boy was blowing up more boulders. "But now it's over, and I'm going home. This is all—I don't know. It's all too *weird* for me! I'm telling you, I can't *do* that kind of thing. You're looking at the wrong person."

"We looked at all your cousins first," Grandma Harman said. "Thea and Blaise. Gillian, who was a lost witch like yourself. Even poor Sylvia, who was seduced over to the enemy side. But it was none of them. Then we found you." She leaned forward, trying to hold Iliana with her eyes. "You have to accept it, child. It's a great responsibility and a great burden, but no one else can do it for you. Come and take your place with us."

Iliana wasn't listening.

It was as simple as that. Keller could almost see the words bouncing off her. And her eyes . . .

Not a veil, Keller thought. A *wall* had dropped down. It had slammed into place, and Iliana was hiding behind it.

"If I don't get home soon, my mother's going to go crazy. I just ran out for a few minutes to get some gold stretchy ribbon—you know, the kind that has like a rubber band inside? It seems like I'm always looking for that. We have some from last year, but it's already tied, and it won't fit on the presents I'm doing."

Keller stared at her, then cast a glance heavenward. She

could see the others staring, too. Winnie's mouth was hanging open. Nissa's eyebrows were in her hair. Galen looked dismayed.

Grandma Harman said, "If you won't accept your responsibilities as a Wild Power, will you at least do your duty as the Witch Child? The winter solstice is next Saturday. On that night, there's going to be a meeting of the shapeshifters and the witches. If we can show them a promise ceremony between you and the son of the First House of the shapeshifters, the shapeshifters will join us."

Keller half expected Iliana to explode. And in the deepest recesses of her own heart, she wouldn't really have blamed her. She could understand Iliana losing it and saying, *What do you think you're doing, waltzing in and trying to hitch me up to some guy I've never met? Asking me to fight is one thing, but ordering me to marry—giving me away like some object—that's another.*

But Iliana didn't say anything like that. She said, "And I've still got so many presents to wrap, and I'm not anywhere near done shopping. Plus, this week at school is going to be completely crazy. And Saturday, that's the night Jaime and Brett Ashton-Hughes are having their birthday party. I can't miss that."

Keller lost it.

"What is wrong with you? Are you deaf or just stupid?"

Iliana talked right over her. "They're twins, you know. And I think Brett kind of likes me. Their family is really rich, and they live in this big house, and they only invite a few people to their parties. All the girls have crushes on him. Brett, I mean."

"No," Keller answered her own question. "You're just the most selfish, spoiled little brat I've ever met!"

"Keller," Nissa said quietly. 'It's no good. The harder you push her, the more she goes into denial."

Keller let out her breath. She knew that it was true, but she had never been more frustrated in her life.

Grandma Harman's face suddenly looked very old and very tired. "Child, we can't force you to do anything. But you have to realize that we're not the only ones who want you. The other side knows about you, too. They won't give up, and they *will* use force."

"And they've got a lot of force." Keller turned to the old woman. "I need to tell you about that. I didn't want to say it on the phone, but they already tried to get Iliana once today. We had to fight them at the mall." She took a deep breath. "And they had a dragon."

Grandma Harman's head jerked up. Those steely lavender-gray eyes fixed on Keller. "Tell me."

Keller told everything. As she did, Grandma Harman's face seemed to get older and older, sinking into haggard lines of worry and sadness. But all she said at the end was, "I see. We'll have to try to find out how they got him, and what exactly his powers are. I don't think there's anybody alive today who's an expert on—those creatures."

"They called him Azhdeha."

"Hmm—sounds Persian."

"It is," Galen said. "It's one of the old names for the constellation Draco. It means 'man-eating serpent.'"

Keller looked at him in surprise. He had been sitting quietly all this time, listening without interrupting. Now he was leaning forward, his gold-green eyes intense.

"The shapeshifters have some old scrolls about dragons. I think you should ask for them. They might give some idea about what powers they have and how to fight them. I saw the scrolls once, but I didn't really study them; I don't think anybody has."

He'd seen the ancient scrolls? Then he *was* a shapeshifter, after all. But why hadn't she been able to sense an animal form for him?

"Galen—" Keller began, but Grandma Harman was speaking.

"It's a good idea. When I get them, I'll send copies to you and Keller. He's one of your people, after all, and you may be able to help figure out how to fight him."

Keller wanted to say indignantly that he wasn't any connection to her, but of course it wasn't true. The dragons had ruled the shapeshifters, once. Their blood still ran in the First House, the Drache family that ruled the shapeshifters today. Whatever that monster was, he *was* one of her people.

"So it's decided. Keller, you and your team will take Iliana home. I'll go back to Circle Daybreak and try to find out more about dragons. Unless . . ." She looked at Iliana. "Unless this discussion has changed your mind."

Iliana, unbelievably, was still prattling, having a conversation about presents with nobody in particular. It was clear that her mind hadn't changed. What wasn't clear to Keller was whether she *had* a mind.

But Keller had other things to worry about.

"I'm sorry—but you're not serious, are you? About taking her home?"

"Perfectly serious," Grandma Harman said.

"But we *can't.*"

"We can, and we have to. You three girls will be her bodyguards—and her friends. I'm hoping that you can persuade her to accept her responsibility by Saturday night at midnight, when the shapeshifters and the witches convene. But if not . . ." Grandma Harman bowed her head slightly, leaning on her cane. She was looking at Iliana. "If not," she said in a barely audible voice, "you'll just have to protect her for as long as you can."

Keller was choking. "I don't see how we can protect her at all. With all respect, ma'am, it's an insane idea. They have to know where her house is by now. Even if we stick beside her twenty-four hours a day—and I don't see how we can even do *that*, with her family around—"

The white head came up, and there was even a faint curve to the old woman's lips. "I'll take care of that. I'll have a talk with her mother—young Anna, Elspeth's granddaughter. I'll introduce myself and explain that her daughter's long-lost cousins' have come to visit for Christmas."

And undoubtedly do something witchy to Anna's mind, Keller thought. Yeah, after that they'd be accepted, although none of them looked a bit like Iliana's cousins.

"And then *I* will put up wards around that house." There was a flash like silver lightning in Grandma Harman's eyes as she said it. "Wards that will hold against anything from the outside. As long as nobody inside disturbs them, you'll be safe." She cocked an eyebrow at Keller. "Satisfied?"

"I'm sorry—no. It's still too dangerous."

"Then what would you suggest we do?"

"Kidnap her," Keller said instantly. She could hear Iliana stop babbling in the background; she wasn't gaining any Brownie points there. She bulldozed on grimly. "Look, I'm just a grunt; I obey orders. But I think that she's too important for us to just let her run around loose where *they* might get hold of her. I think we should take her to a Circle Daybreak enclave like the ones where the other Wild Powers are. Where we can protect her from the enemy."

Grandma Harman looked her in the eye. "If we do that," she said mildly, "then we *are* the enemy."

There was a pause. Keller said, "With all respect, ma'am—"

"I don't want your respect. I want your obedience. The leaders of Circle Daybreak made a firm decision when this whole thing started. If we can't convince a Wild Power by reasoning, we will not resort to force. So your orders are to take your team and stay with this child and protect her as long as you can."

"Excuse me." It was Galen. The others had been sitting and watching silently. Nissa and Winnie were too smart to get involved in an exchange like this, but Keller could see that they were both unhappy.

"What is it?" Grandma Harman asked.

"If you don't mind, I'd like to go with them. I could be another 'cousin.' It would make four of us to watch over her—better odds."

Keller thought she might have an apoplexy.

She was so mad, she couldn't even get words out. While she was choking uselessly, Galen was going on. His face still looked pale and strained, like a young soldier coming back from battle, but his dark gold hair was shining, and his eyes were steady. His whole attitude was one of earnest pleading.

"I'm not a fighter, but maybe I can learn. After all, that's what we're asking Iliana to do, isn't it? Can we ask anything of her that we're not ready to do ourselves?"

Grandma Harman, who had been frowning, now looked him up and down appraisingly. "You have a fine young mind," she said. "Like your father's. He and your mother were both strong warriors, as well."

Galen's eyes darkened. "I'd hoped I wouldn't have to be one. But it looks like we can't always choose."

Keller didn't know what they were talking about or why the Crone of all the Witches knew the parents of this guy she'd met in a mall. But she'd finally gotten the obstruction out of her throat.

"No way!" she said explosively. She was on her feet now, too, black hair flying as she looked from Grandma Harman to Galen. "I mean it. There is *no way* I am taking this boy back with us. And you may be the leader of the witches, ma'am, but, no offense intended, I don't think you have the authority to make me. I'd have to hear it from the leaders of Circle Daybreak themselves, from Thierry Descouedres or Lady Hannah. Or from the First House of the shapeshifters."

Grandma Harman gave an odd snort. Keller ignored it. "It's not just that he's not a fighter. He's not *involved* in this. He doesn't have any part in it."

Grandma Harman looked at Galen, not entirely approvingly. "It seems you've been keeping secrets. Are you going to tell her, or shall I?"

"I—" Galen turned from her to Keller. "Listen. I'm sorry—I should have mentioned it before." His eyes were embarrassed and apologetic. "It just—there just didn't seem to be a right time." He winced. "I wasn't in that mall today accidentally. I came by to look for Iliana. I wanted to see her, maybe get to know her a little."

Keller stared at him, not breathing. "Why?"

"Because . . ." He winced again. "I'm Galen Drache . . . of the First House of the shapeshifters."

Keller blinked while the room revolved briefly.

I should have known. I should have *realized.* That's why he seemed like a shapeshifter, but I couldn't get any animal sense from him.

Children of the First House weren't born connected to any particular animal. They had power over all animals, and they were allowed to choose when they became adults which one they would shift into.

It also explained how he'd known which pressure points to use to get her off the dragon. And his telepathy—children of the First House could connect to any animal mind.

When the room settled back into place, Keller realized that she was still standing there, and Galen was still looking at her. His eyes were almost beseeching.

"I should have explained," he said.

"Well, of course, it was your choice," Keller said stiffly. There was an unusual amount of blood in her cheeks; she could feel it burning. She went on, "And, naturally, I'm sorry if anything I've said has given offense."

"Keller, please don't be formal."

"Let's see, I haven't greeted you properly, or given you my obedience." Keller took his hand, which was well made, long-fingered, and cold. She brought it to her forehead. "Welcome,

Drache, son of the First House of the shapeshifters. I'm yours to command, naturally."

There was a silence. Keller dropped Galen's hand. Galen looked miserable.

"You're *really* mad now, aren't you?" he observed.

"I wish you every happiness with your new bride," Keller said through her teeth.

She couldn't figure out exactly *why* she was so mad. Sure, she'd been made a fool of, and now she was going to have to take responsibility for an untrained boy who couldn't even shapeshift into a mouse. But it was more than that.

He's going to marry that whiny little flower in the corner, a voice in Keller's head whispered. He *has* to marry her, or at least go through a promise ceremony that's just as binding as marriage. If he doesn't, the shapeshifters will never join with the witches. They've said so, and they'll never back down. And if they don't join with the witches . . . everything you've ever worked for is finished.

And your job is to persuade the flower to do her duty, the voice continued brightly. That means you've got to convince her to marry him. Instead of eating her.

Keller's temper flared. I don't want to eat her, she snapped back at the voice. And I don't care who this idiot marries. It's none of my business.

She realized that the room was still silent, and everyone

was watching Iliana and Galen. Iliana had stopped prattling. She was looking at Galen with huge violet eyes. He was looking back, strained and serious.

Then he turned to Keller again. "I'd still like to help, if you'll let me come."

"I told you, I'm yours to command," Keller said shortly. "It's your decision. I'd like to mention that it just makes things a little harder on my team. Now we're going to have to look out for you as well as her. Because, you see, you're *not* expendable after all."

"I don't want you to look out for me," he said soberly. "I'm not important."

Keller wanted to say, Don't be an idiot. No you, no promise ceremony, no treaty. It's as simple as that. We've *got* to protect you. But she'd already said more than enough.

Toby was retrieving the tape from the VCR. Grandma Harman was making getting-ready-to-rise motions with her cane. "I think we've stayed here long enough," she said to Keller.

Keller nodded stiffly. "Would you like to come in the limo? Or would you rather follow us to her house?"

Grandma Harman opened her mouth to answer, but she never got the chance. Keller's ears caught the sound of movement outside just before the living room window shattered.

CHAPTER 6

It was a full-force invasion. Even before the echoes of breaking glass had died, figures in black uniforms were swarming through the window.

Dark ninjas, Keller thought. An elite group made up of vampires and shapeshifters, the Night World experts at sneaking and killing.

Keller's mind, which had been roiling in clouds of stifled anger, was suddenly crystal clear.

"Nissa, take her!" she shouted. It was all she needed to say. Nissa grabbed Iliana. It didn't matter that Iliana was screaming breathlessly and too shocked to want to go anywhere. Nissa was a vampire and stronger than a human Olympic weight lifter. She simply picked Iliana up and ran with her toward the back door.

Without being told, Winfrith followed close behind, orange energy already sizzling between her palms. Keller knew she would provide good cover—Winnie was a fighting witch. She made full use of the new powers that all the Night People were developing as the millennium got closer. As one of the ninjas lunged after them, she let loose with a blast of poppy-colored energy that knocked him sideways.

"Now you!" Keller shouted to Galen, trying to hustle him into the hallway without turning from the ninjas. She hadn't changed and didn't want to if she could avoid it. Changing took time, left you vulnerable for the few seconds that you were between forms. Right now seconds counted.

Galen got a few steps down the hall, then stopped. "Grandma Harman!"

I knew it, Keller thought. He's a liability.

The old woman was still in the living room, standing with her feet braced apart, cane ready. Her apprentice, Toby, was in front of her, working up some witch incantation and tossing energy. They were right in the flow of the ninjas.

Which was as it ought to be. Keller's mind had clicked through the possibilities right at the beginning and had come to the only reasonable conclusion.

"We have to leave her!"

Galen turned to her, his face lit by the multicolored energy that was flying around them. *"What?"*

"She's too slow! We have to protect you and Iliana. Get moving!"

His features were etched in shock. "You're joking. Just wait here—*I'll* bring her."

"No! Galen—"

He was already running back.

Keller cursed.

"Go on!" she yelled to Nissa and Winnie, who were at the entrance to the kitchen, where the back door was. "Take the limo if you can get to it. Don't wait for us!"

Then she turned and plunged into the living room.

Galen was trying to shield Grandma Harman from the worst of the energy being exchanged. Keller gritted her teeth. This group of ninjas was only the first wave. They were here to breach the wards and make an opening for whatever was going to follow.

Which could be a dragon.

The ninjas hadn't finished their job, though. Most of the wards were holding, and the one that had fallen was on a small window. The dark figures could only squirm in one at a time. The house shook as whoever was outside slammed power at it, trying to break a bigger entrance.

Faintly, Keller heard an engine rev up outside. She hoped it was the limo.

Galen was pulling at Grandma Harman. Toby was grappling hand-to-hand with a ninja.

Keller batted a couple of the sneaks out of her way. She wasn't trying to kill them, just put them out of commission. She had almost reached Galen.

And then she heard the rumbling.

Only her panther ears could have picked it up. Just as the

first time when she'd heard it, it was so deep that it seemed both soft and frighteningly loud. It shook her to her bones.

In a flash, she knew what was coming.

And there was no time to think about what to do.

Galen seemed to have sensed it, too. Keller saw him looking at the roof just above the door. Then he turned toward Grandma Harman, shouting.

After that, everything happened at once. Galen knocked the old woman down and fell on top of her. At the same time, Keller sprang and landed on top of both of them.

She was changing even as she did it. Changing and spreading herself out, trying to make herself as wide and flat as possible. A panther rug to cover them.

The brick wall exploded just as the window had, only louder.

Shattered with Power, Keller thought. The dragon had recovered . . . fast.

And then it was raining bricks. One hit Keller in the leg, and she lashed her tail in fury. Another struck her back, and she felt a deep pain. Then one got her in the head, and she saw white light. She could hear Galen shouting under her. It seemed to be her name.

Then nothing.

Something wet touched her face. Keller hissed automatically, pawing at it in annoyance.

"Lemme 'lone."

"Boss, wake up. Come on, it's morning already."

Keller opened heavy eyes.

She was dreaming. She had to be. Either that, or the after-life was full of teenage girls. Winnie was bending over her with a dripping washcloth, and Nissa was peering critically over her shoulder. Behind Nissa was Iliana's anxious little heart-shaped face, her hair falling like two shimmering curtains of silvery-starlight gold on either side.

Keller blinked. "I was sure I was dead."

"Well, you got close," Winnie said cheerfully. "Me and Toby and Grandma Harman have been working on you most of the night. You're going to be kind of stiff, but I guess your skull was too thick to crack."

Keller sat up and was rewarded with a stabbing pain in her temples. "What happened? Where's Galen?"

"Well, golly gee, Boss, I didn't know you cared—"

"Stop fooling around, Winnie! Where's the guy who's got to be alive if the shapeshifters are going to join Circle Daybreak?"

Winnie sobered. Nissa said calmly, "He's fine, Keller. This is Iliana's house. Everybody's okay. We got you guys out—"

Keller frowned, struck by a new worry. "You did? Why? I told you to take the girl and go."

Nissa raised an eyebrow wryly. "Yes, well, but the girl didn't want to go. She made us stop and turn back for you."

"For Galen," Keller said. She looked at Iliana, who was

wearing a pink nightgown with puffy sleeves and looked about seven. She tried to make her voice patient. "It was good to think of him, but you should have followed the plan."

"Anyway, it worked out," Nissa said. "Apparently, the dragon blew the house down on top of you, but then he walked right over you trying to get to us."

"Yeah. I was kind of hoping he wouldn't realize Galen was there," Keller said. "Or wouldn't realize he was important."

"Well, when he found we'd already gotten away in the limo, he and his buddies took after us in cars," Winnie said. "But Nissa lost them. And then Iliana . . . insisted, and so we circled back. And there you were. Galen and Toby were digging you out. We helped them and brought you here."

"What about Grandma Harman?"

"She came out of it without a scratch. She's tougher than she looks," Winnie said.

"She talked to Iliana's mom last night," Nissa added. "She fixed everything up so we can stay here. You're supposed to be a distant cousin, and the rest of us are your friends. We're from Canada. We graduated last year, and we're touring the U.S. by bus. We ran into Iliana last night, and that's why she was late. It's all covered, nice and neat."

"It's all ludicrous," Keller said. She looked at Iliana. "And it's time to stop. Haven't you seen enough yet? That's twice you've been attacked by a monster. Do you really want to try your luck for a third time?"

It was a mistake. Iliana's face had been sweet and anxious, but now Keller could see the walls slam down. The violet eyes hazed over and sparked at the same time.

"*Nobody* attacked me until you guys came!" Iliana flared. "In fact, nobody's attacked *me* so far at all. I think it's you people they're after—or maybe Galen. I keep telling you that I'm not the one you're looking for."

This was the time for diplomacy, but Keller was too exasperated to think. "You don't really believe that. Unless you *practice* being stupid—"

"Stop calling me stupid!" The last word was a piercing shriek. At the same time, Iliana threw something at Keller. She batted it out of the air automatically before it could hit.

"I'm not stupid! And I'm not your Witch Child or whatever you call it! I'm just a normal kid, and I like my life. And if I can't live my life, then I don't want to—to do *anything*." She whirled around and stalked out, her nightgown billowing.

Keller stared at the missile she'd caught. It was a stuffed lamb with outrageously long eyelashes and a pink ribbon tied around its white neck.

Nissa folded her arms. "Well, you sure handled that one, Boss."

"Give me a break." Keller tossed the lamb onto the window seat. "And just how did she *make* you two turn around and come back for us, by the way?

Winnie pursed her lips. "You heard it. Volume control.

She kept screaming like—well, I don't know *what* screams like that. You'd be surprised how effective it is."

"You're agents of Circle Daybreak; you're supposed to be immune to torture." But Keller dropped the subject. "What are you still hanging around for?" she added, as she swung her feet out of bed and carefully tried her legs. "You're supposed to stick with her, even when she's in the house. Don't stand here staring at *me.*"

"You're welcome for putting you back together again," Winnie said, her eyes on the ceiling. In the doorway, she turned and added, "And, you know, it wasn't Galen she kept screaming we had to go back and get last night. It was you, Keller."

Keller stared at the door as it shut, bewildered.

"You can't go to school," Keller hissed. "Do you hear me? You cannot go to school."

They were all sitting around the kitchen table. Iliana's mother, a lovely woman with a knot of platinum hair coiled on her neck, was making breakfast. She seemed slightly anxious about her four new houseguests, but in a pleasantly excited way. She certainly wasn't suspicious. Grandma Harman had done a good job of brainwashing.

"We're going to have a wonderful Christmas," she said now, and her angelic smile grew brighter. "We can go into

Winston-Salem for a Christmas and Candle Tea. Have you ever had a Moravian sugar-cake? I just wish Great-Aunt Edgith had been able to stay."

Grandma Harman was gone. Keller didn't know whether to be relieved or frustrated. Despite what she kept saying, as long as the old woman was around, Keller would worry about her. But with her gone, there was nobody to appeal to, nobody who could order Iliana into safekeeping.

So now they were sitting and having this argument. It looked like such a normal breakfast scene, Keller thought dryly. Iliana's father had already left for work. Her mother was bustling around cheerfully. Her little brother was in a high chair making a mess with Cheerios. Too bad that the four nicely dressed teenagers at the table were actually two shapeshifters, a witch, and a vampire.

Galen was directly opposite Keller. There were shadows under his eyes—had anyone gotten any sleep last night?—and he seemed subdued but relaxed. Keller hadn't had a chance to speak to him since the dragon's attack.

Not that she had anything to say.

"Orange juice, Kelly?"

"No, thank you, Mrs. Dominick." That was what this family thought their last name was. They didn't realize that witches trace their heritage through the female line and that both Iliana and her mother were therefore Harmans.

"Oh, please, call me Aunt Anna," the woman said. She had her daughter's violet eyes and the smile of an angel. She was also pouring Keller juice.

Now I see where Iliana gets her scintillating intelligence, Keller thought. "Oh—thanks, Aunt Anna. And, actually, it's Keller, not Kelly."

"How unusual. But it's nice, so modern."

"It's my last name, but that's what everybody calls me."

"Oh, really? What's your first name?"

Keller broke off a piece of toast, feeling uncomfortable. "Raksha."

"But that's beautiful! Why don't you use it?"

Keller shrugged. "I just don't." She could see Galen looking at her. Shapeshifters usually were named for their animal forms, but neither *Keller* nor *Raksha* fit the pattern. "I was abandoned as a kid," she said in a clipped voice, looking back at Galen. Iliana's mother wouldn't be able to make anything of this, but she might as well satisfy the princeling's curiosity. "So I don't know my real last name. But my first name means 'demon.'"

Iliana's mother paused with the juice carton over Nissa's glass. "Oh. How . . . nice. Well, then, I see." She blinked a couple of times and walked off without pouring Nissa any juice.

"So what does *Galen* mean?" Keller said, holding his gaze challengingly and handing her full glass to Nissa.

He smiled—a little wryly—for the first time since sitting down. "'Calm.'"

Keller snorted. "It figures."

"I like *Raksha* better."

Keller didn't answer. With "Aunt Anna" safely in the kitchen, she could speak again to Iliana. "You understood before, right? That you can't go to school."

"I have to go to school." For somebody who looked as if she were made of spun glass, Iliana ate a lot. She spoke around a mouthful of microwave pancake.

"It's out of the question. How can we go with you? What are we supposed to *be*, for Goddess's sake?"

"My long-lost cousin from Canada and her friends," Iliana said indistinctly. "Or you can all be exchange students who're here to study our American educational system." Before Keller could say anything, she added, "Hey, how come *you* guys aren't at school? Don't you have schools?"

"We've got the same ones you do," Winnie said. "Except Nissa—she graduated last year. But Keller and I are seniors like you. We just take time off for this stuff."

"I bet your grades are as bad as mine," Iliana said unemotionally. "Anyway, I have to go to school this week. There are all sorts of class parties and things. You can come. It'll be fun."

Keller wanted to hit her with the pot of grits.

She had a problem, though. Iliana's little brother Alex had escaped from his high chair and was climbing up her leg. She looked down at him uneasily. She wasn't good with family-type things, and she especially wasn't good with children.

"Okay," she said. "Go on back and sit down." She peeled him off and tried to start him in the right direction.

He turned around and put his arms up. "Kee-kee. Kee-kee."

"That's his word for 'kitty,'" Iliana's mother said, coming in with a plate of sausages. She ruffled his white-blond hair. "You mean Kelly, Kelly," she told him.

"'Keller, Keller,'" Winnie corrected helpfully.

Alex climbed into Keller's lap, grabbed her hair, and hoisted himself into a standing position. She found herself looking into huge violet baby eyes. Witch eyes.

"Kee-kee," he said flatly, and gave her a sloppy kiss on the cheek.

Winnie grinned. "Having trouble?"

The kid had two chubby arms around Keller's neck now and was nudging her chin with his head like a kitten looking for pets. He had a good grip, too. This time, she couldn't peel him off.

"It's just—distracting," she said, giving up and petting him awkwardly. It was ridiculous. How could she argue with baby giggles in her ears?

"You look kind of sweet together," Iliana observed. "I'm getting dressed for school now. You guys can do whatever you want."

She floated off while Keller was trying to think of a reply.

Nissa and Winnie hastily followed her. Galen got up to help Iliana's mother with the dishes.

Keller tugged at the baby, who clung like a sloth. Maybe there was shapeshifter blood in this family.

"Kee-kee . . . pui!" That was what it sounded like.

"Pwee?" Keller glanced nervously at his diaper.

"He means 'pretty,'" Iliana's mother said, coming back in. "It's funny. He doesn't usually take to people like that. He likes animals better."

"Oh. Well, he has good taste," Keller said. She finally succeeded in detaching him and gave him back to his mother. Then she started down the hallway after Iliana, muttering, "Too bad about his eyesight."

"I think his eyesight's just fine," Galen said, right behind her.

Keller turned, realizing they were alone in the hall.

His faint smile faded. "I really wanted to talk to you," he said.

CHAPTER 7

Keller faced him squarely.

"Yes, sir? Or should I say 'my lord'?"

He flinched but tried to hide it. "I should have told you in the beginning."

Keller wasn't about to get into a discussion of it. "What do you want?"

"Can we go in there?" He nodded toward what looked like a small library-office combination.

Keller didn't want to, but she couldn't think of any acceptable reason to refuse. She followed him and crossed her arms when he closed the door.

"You saved my life." He wasn't quite facing her; he was looking out the window at a cold silver sky. Against it, he had a profile like a young prince on an ancient coin.

Keller shrugged. "Maybe. Maybe not. The bricks didn't kill me; maybe they wouldn't have killed you."

"But you were trying to save my life. I did something that was probably stupid—again—and you had to cover for me."

"I did it because it's my job, Galen. That's what I *do.*"

"You got hurt because of me. When I dug myself out of that rubble, I thought you *were* dead." He said it flatly, without any particular intonation. But the hairs on Keller's arms rose.

"I've got to get back to Iliana."

"Keller."

There was something wrong with her. She was facing the door, heading out, but his voice stopped her in her tracks.

"Keller. Please."

She was aware that he was coming up behind her.

Her entire skin was up in gooseflesh. She was *too* aware of him, that was the problem. She could feel the air that he displaced. She could feel his heat.

He just stood there.

"Keller. Ever since I first saw you . . ." He stopped and tried again. "You were—gleaming. All that long black hair swirling around you and those silvery eyes. And then you changed. I don't think I ever really understood what it meant to be a shapeshifter until I saw that. You were a girl and then you were a cat, but you were always both." He let out his breath. "I'm putting this badly."

Keller needed to think of something to say—*now.* But she couldn't, and she couldn't seem to move.

"When I saw that, for the first time, I wanted to shapeshift. Before that, I didn't really care, and everyone was always telling me to be careful, because whatever shape I choose the first time is the one I'm stuck with. But that's not what I'm trying to say. I'm trying . . ."

He reached out. Keller felt the warmth of his hand between her shoulder blades, through her hair, through the fabric of her spare jumpsuit.

Keller shivered.

She couldn't help it. She felt so strange. Dizzy and supernaturally clear at the same time. Weak.

She didn't know what was happening to her, only that it was powerful and terrible.

His hand remained on her back, warmth from it soaking into her skin.

"I realize how much you dislike me," Galen said quietly. There was no self-pity in his voice, but he seemed to be getting the words out painfully. "And I'm not going to try to change that. But I just wanted you to know, I also realize what you've done for me. I needed to say thank you." There was something swelling in Keller's chest like a balloon. Bigger and bigger. She clamped her lips together, frightened as she had never been when fighting monsters.

"And . . . I won't forget it," Galen was going on, still quiet. "Someday, I'll find a way to repay you."

Keller felt desperate. What was he *doing* to her? She wasn't in control of herself; she was trembling and terrified that the thing in her chest was going to escape.

All she could imagine doing was turning around and hitting him, like a trapped animal lashing out at someone trying to rescue it.

"It's so strange," he said, and Keller had the feeling that he had almost forgotten her and was talking to himself. "When I was growing up, I rejected the Power of my family. All my ancestors, they were supposed to turn into demons when they unleashed it. I thought that it was better not to fight—if that was possible. It seems unrealistic now."

Keller could feel more than warmth now. There were little electrical zings spreading out from his hand, running down the insides of her arms. Not real ones, of course. Not the Power he was talking about, like the Power used by the dragon or Winnie. But it felt awfully close. Her whole body was filled with buzzing.

Some people shouldn't have to fight, she thought giddily. But, no, that was insane. Everybody had to fight; that was what life was about. If you didn't fight, you were weak. You were prey.

He was still talking in that abstracted tone. "I know you think—"

Keller's panic hit flashpoint. She whirled around. "You don't know *anything* about what I think. You don't know anything about *me.* I don't know whatever gave you the idea that you did."

He looked startled but not defensive. The silver light behind him lit the edges of his fine hair.

"I'm sorry," he said gently.

"Stop being sorry!"

"Are you saying I'm wrong? You don't think I'm a spoiled and pampered prince who doesn't know anything about real life and has to be babysat?"

Keller was disconcerted. That was exactly what she thought—but if it were true, then why did she have this strange feeling of falling?

"I think you're like *her*," she said, keeping her words short and brutal to keep them under control. She didn't need to specify the *her*. "You're like this whole ridiculous family. Happy mommy, happy baby, happy Christmas. They're ready to love everybody who comes along. And they're living in a happy happy idealistic world that has nothing to do with reality."

The corner of his mouth turned up wryly, although his eyes were still serious. "I think that's what I said."

"And it sounds harmless, doesn't it? But it isn't. It's blind and destructive. What do you want to bet that Iliana's mother really thinks my name is Kelly now? She can't deal with it being 'demon,' so she just happily changes the world to fit."

"You could be right." He wasn't smiling at all now, and there was something in his eyes, something lost and hopeless that made Keller feel more panicked than ever.

She spoke savagely to hold off the fear. "You want to know

what real life is like? My mother left me in a cardboard box in a parking lot. It was fixed up with newspapers inside, like something you'd use for a puppy. That was because I couldn't wear diapers, I was stuck in my halfway form—a baby with a tail and ears like a cat. Maybe that was why she couldn't deal with me, but I'll never know. The only thing I have of hers is a note that was in the box. I kept it."

Keller fumbled in the jumpsuit's pocket. She had never meant to show this to anyone, certainly not somebody she'd known for less than twenty-four hours. But she had to convince Galen; she had to make him go away for good.

Her wallet was slim—no photos, just money and ID. She pulled out a folded slip of paper, with creases worn smooth by time and writing that had faded from blue ink to pale purple. Its right edge was a ragged tear, but the words were on the left and clear enough.

"It was her legacy to me," Keller said. "She was trying to pass on the truth, what she'd learned about life."

Galen took the paper as if it were a hurt bird.

Keller watched his eyes move over it. She knew the words by heart, of course, and right now she heard them ringing in her mind. There were only twelve of them—her mother had been a master of succinctness.

People die . . .
Beauty fades . . .

Love changes . . .
And you will always be alone.

Keller could tell where Galen was by the way his eyes widened in horror.

She smiled at him, not nicely, and took the paper back.

He looked at her. And despite everything she knew about him, she was surprised at the sheer *depth* of his shock. He stared at her with those gold-green eyes that went on for miles—and then he stepped forward.

"You don't believe that," he said fiercely, and grabbed her by the shoulders.

Keller was startled. He'd seen her in action. How could he be so stupid as to grab her?

He seemed to be completely unaware of his danger. There was nothing calm or hesitant about him now. He was staring at her with a kind of stricken tenderness, as if she'd just told him she had a terminal disease. It was as if he were trying to pour love and warmth and light into her by a direct connection.

"I won't let you think that," he said. "I won't let you."

"It's just the truth. If you can accept that, you won't drown in life. Whatever happens, you'll be able to cope."

"It's not all the truth. If you believe it is, why do you work for Circle Daybreak?"

"They raised me," Keller said shortly. "They snatched me out of the hospital nursery when they read the reports about me in the paper. They realized what I was and that humans couldn't take care of me. That's why I work for them—to pay them back. It's my job."

"That's not the only reason. I've *seen* you work, Keller."

She could feel warmth spreading from his hands on her shoulders. She knocked them aside and stood tall. There was a core of iciness inside her, and she hung on to that.

"Don't get me wrong," she said. "I don't save people out of idealism. I don't risk my neck for just *anybody*—only the ones I get paid for."

"You mean if Iliana's little brother was in danger, you wouldn't save him. You'd stand there and watch him burn to death in a fire or drown in a riptide."

Keller had a sinking feeling. She held her chin up and said, "Exactly. If it meant putting myself in danger to save him, I wouldn't do it."

He shook his head, flatly positive. "No."

The sinking feeling got worse.

"That's a lie," he said, holding her eyes. "I've seen you in action. I talked to Nissa and Winnie last night. And I've seen your *mind.* You're not just doing a job. You're doing what you do because you think it's right. And you are . . ." He paused as if to find the words, then spoke deliberately. "You are the soul of honor."

And you're insane, Keller thought. She *really* needed to get away now. The sinking was becoming a terrible weakness spreading through her. And although she knew that what he was saying was complete garbage, she couldn't seem to stop listening.

"You put on a good show," Galen said, "but the truth is that you're brave and gallant and *decent.* You have your own code, and you would never break it. And anybody who knows you sees that. Don't you know what your team thinks of you? You should have seen their faces—and Iliana's—when they thought you were dead in that rubble. Your soul is straight as a sword, and you have more honor than anyone I've ever known."

His eyes were the color of the first new leaves in spring, the kind you look up to see sunlight pouring through. Keller was a meat-eater and had never cared much about flowers or other vegetation, but now she remembered a line from a poem, and it froze in her mind like lightning: *Nature's first green is gold.* This was the color the poet meant.

You could drown in eyes like that.

He was holding her arms again. He couldn't seem to stop reaching for her, as if she were some soul in danger of being lost forever.

"Your life's been so hard. You deserve to have good things happen to you now—only good things. I wish . . ." He broke off, and a sort of tremor went through his face.

No, Keller thought. I won't let you make me weak. I won't listen to your lies.

But the problem was that Galen *didn't* lie. He was one of those idiot idealist types who said what they believed. And she shouldn't care what he believed, but she found that she did. She cared terribly.

Galen just stood there looking at her with tears in his gem-bright eyes.

Something ripped inside Keller. And then everything changed.

Keller couldn't understand what was happening at first. In panic, all she could think was that she was losing herself. Losing her armor, her hardness, everything she needed to keep alive. Some part of her deep inside was melting, flowing toward Galen.

She tried to snatch it back, but it was no good. She couldn't stop it.

With a distant shock, she realized that she had shut her eyes. She was falling, falling—and she didn't care.

Something caught her.

She felt the warmth of arms around her, supporting her. And she felt herself lean into it, relaxing, letting him take some of her weight, as if someone else were controlling her body.

So warm . . .

That was when Keller discovered something strange. That warmth could give you shivers.

Being close like this, feeling Galen warm and solid and there to hang on to—it made a shiver of pleasure go through her.

And then she felt the true connection.

It wasn't a physical thing. The spark that passed between them connected them mind to mind. It was a riveting flash of complete understanding.

Her heart all but exploded.

It's you. The voice was in her mind, the same voice she'd heard yesterday when he had tried to save her from the dragon. It was filled with wonder and discovery. *It's you . . . the one I've been looking for. You're the one . . .*

And Keller would have told him how insane that was, except that it was just what she was feeling herself. It was as if she had just turned around and unexpectedly found herself facing a figure from one of her dreams. A person she *knew* instinctively, just as she knew her own mind.

I know you, too, Galen's voice in her head said. *We're so much alike . . .*

We're not, Keller thought. But the protest sounded feeble even to her. And trying to hang on to her anger and cynicism right now seemed silly—pointless. Like a kid insisting that nobody loved her and she was going to go play on the freeway.

We belong together, Galen said simply. *Like this.*

Warm tingles. Keller could feel the force of his love like a bright light shining at her. And she couldn't . . . resist . . . any longer . . .

Her arms came up to hold Galen back. Her face turned up

slightly, but not much, because she was tall, and their lips were already only an inch apart.

The kiss was shivery, delightful, and very sweet.

After an endless time of floating in a golden haze, Keller shivered again.

There's something . . . something I have to remember . . .

I love you, Galen said back.

Yes, but there's something I've forgotten . . .

We're together, he said. *I don't want to remember anything else.*

And *that* was probably true. She couldn't really blame him. Who would want to disturb this warmth and closeness and quiet joy?

Still, they had been talking about something—a long time ago, when she had been alone. Something that had made her terribly unhappy.

I won't let you be unhappy. I won't let you be alone, either, he said.

He stroked her hair with his fingertips. That was all, but it almost short-circuited Keller's thought processes.

But not completely.

Alone . . . I remember.

Her mother's note.

You will always be alone.

Galen's arms tightened around her. *Don't. Don't think about that. We're together. I love you . . .*

No.

With a wrench, Keller pulled herself away. She found herself standing in the library on her own two feet, staring at Galen. He looked shocked and stricken, as if he'd just been slapped out of a dream.

"Keller—"

"No!" she spat. "Don't touch me!"

"I won't touch you. But I can't let you run away. And I can't pretend I don't love you."

"Love," Keller snarled, "is weakness." She saw her mother's note lying on the floor where he'd dropped it, and snatched it up. "And nobody is making me sentimental and weak! Nobody!"

It wasn't until she was out the door that she remembered she had left out the strongest argument of all.

He *couldn't* love her. It was impossible.

He was destined to marry the Witch Child.

The fate of the world depended on it.

CHAPTER 8

Keller was tempted to check the wards, but she knew it wouldn't do any good. She wasn't sensitive enough to the witch energies to gauge them. They'd been put up by Grandma Harman and checked by Winnie, and she would have to trust to that.

The wards were keyed so that only the Dominick family and ordinary humans could come inside. No Night Person could enter except Nissa, Winnie, Keller, and Galen. Which meant, Keller thought with a grim smile, that any lost witch relatives of Iliana's mother who came by were going to get quite a surprise. An invisible wall was going to be blocking them from crossing the threshold.

As long as nobody on the inside removed the wards, the house was safer than Fort Knox.

Grandma Harman had also taken the limo, Keller found. Sometime during the night, it had been replaced by an inconspicuous Ford sedan parked at the curb. The keys had been in a manila envelope dropped through the mail slot in the front door, along with a map of Lucy Lee Bethea High School.

Circle Daybreak was efficient.

"I didn't finish my *hair*," Iliana complained as Nissa hustled her to the car. "It's only half *done*."

"It looks terrific," Winnie said from behind her.

And the thing was, it was true. There was nothing that could make that shimmering waterfall of silvery-gold look anything less than beautiful. Whether it was up or down, braided or pinned or falling loose, it was glorious.

I don't even think the little nitwit has to brush it, Keller thought. It's so fine that she couldn't make two hairs tangle if she tried.

"And I left my *scarf*—"

"Here it is." Keller lassoed her. The scarf was ridiculous, crushed velvet in muted metallic colors, with a six-inch fringe. Purely decorative.

Iliana choked as Keller wound it around a few times and pulled it tight.

"A little aggressive, Boss?" Winfrith asked, extricating Iliana before she could turn blue.

"Worried about being late," Keller said shortly. But she saw Nissa eyeing her, too.

Galen was the last to come out of the house. He was pale and serious—that much Keller saw before she shifted her eyes past him. Iliana's mother actually remained standing at the door with the baby in her arms.

"Say bye-bye to your sister's friends. Bye-bye."

"Kee-kee," the baby said. "Kee-kee!"

"Wave to him," Winfrith stage-whispered.

Keller gritted her teeth. She half-waved, keeping her senses opened for any sound of an impending attack. The baby held out his arms toward her.

"Pui!"

"Let's get *out* of here." Keller almost shoved Iliana into the backseat.

Nissa took the wheel, and Galen sat up front with her. Winnie ran around to get in the back on the other side of Iliana.

As they pulled out, Keller saw the outside of the house for the first time. It was a nice house—white clapboard, two and a half stories, Colonial Revival. The street was nice, too, lined with dogwoods that would be a mass of white when they bloomed. The sort of street where people sat outside on their rockers in spring and somebody was bound to have a stand of bees in the side yard making sourwood honey.

Although Keller had been all over the United States, sent from one Circle Daybreak group to another, the hospital where she'd been found had been near a neighborhood like this.

I might have grown up someplace like this. If they'd kept me. My parents . . .

Do I *hate* her? Keller wondered suddenly. I couldn't. It's not her fault.

Oh, no, of course not, the voice in her mind said. Not her fault that she's beautiful and perfect and has parents who love her and blue fire in her veins and that she is going to be forced, whether she wants it or not, to marry Galen . . .

Which I don't *care* about, Keller thought. She was shocked at herself. When had she ever let emotion interfere with her job? She was allowing herself to be distracted—she had allowed herself to be distracted all morning—when there was something vitally important at stake.

No more, she told herself fiercely. From now on, I think about nothing but the mission. Years of mental discipline came in handy now; she was able to push everything to the side and focus with icy clarity on what had to be done.

"—stopped a train in its tracks," Winfrith was saying.

"Really?" There was faint interest in Iliana's voice. At least she'd stopped talking about her hair, Keller thought.

"Really. It was one of those BART trains in San Francisco, like a subway train, you know. The two girls were on the tracks, and the Wild Power stopped the train dead before it could hit them. That's what the blue fire can do."

"Well, I know I can't do anything like that," Iliana said

flatly. "So I can't be a Wild Power. Or whatever." The last words were tacked on quickly.

Nissa raised a cool eyebrow. "Have you ever *tried* to stop a train?"

While Iliana bit a fingertip and pondered that, Winnie said, "You have to do it right, you know. First, you have to make blood flow, and then you have to concentrate. It's not something you can expect to do perfectly the very first time."

"If you want to start practicing," Nissa added, "we can help."

Iliana shuddered. "No, thank you. I faint when I see blood. And anyway, I'm not it."

"Too bad," Nissa murmured. "We could use the blue fire on our side today."

They were pulling up to a charming old brown brick high school. Neither Galen nor Keller had said a word throughout the ride.

But now Keller leaned forward. "Nissa, drive past it. I want to check the layout first."

Nissa swung the car into a circular driveway that went past the school's oversized front doors. Keller looked right and left, taking in everything about the surroundings. She could see Winnie doing the same thing—and Galen, too. He was focusing on the same danger spots she was. He had the instinct for strategy.

"Go around the block and circle back," Keller said.

Iliana stirred. "I thought you were worried about me being late."

"I'm more worried about you being dead," Keller interrupted. "What do you think, Nissa?"

"The side door on the west. Easy to pull up reasonably close, no bushes around it for nasty surprises to hide in."

"That's my pick, too. Okay, everybody, listen. Nissa's going to slow the car down in the right place. Slow down, not stop. When I give the signal, we're all going to jump out and go directly to that door. We are not going to pause. We are going to move as a group. Iliana, are you paying attention? From now on, you don't go *anywhere* unless Winnie's in front of you and I'm beside you."

"And where's Galen?" Iliana said.

Keller cursed herself mentally. She wasn't used to working with a fourth team member. "He'll be behind us—okay, Galen?" She made herself look his way.

"Yes. Whatever you say." There wasn't the slightest hint of sarcasm in his face. He was dead serious. Absolutely miserable, earnest, and dead serious.

"And, Nissa, once you've parked, you join us and take the other side. What room's your first class in, Iliana?"

"Three twenty-six," Iliana said dismally. "U.S. History with Mr. Wanamaker. He went to New York to try to be an actor, but all he got was some disease from not eating enough stuff with vitamins. So he came back, and now he's really strict unless you can get him to do his impressions of the presidents—"

"All right," Keller broke in. "We're coming to the door."

"—and he's actually pretty funny when he does Theodore Roosevelt—or do I mean the other one—"

"Now," Keller said, and pushed her as Winnie pulled.

They all made it out smoothly, although Iliana yelped a little. Keller kept a good grip on her arm as they hurried to the door.

"I don't think I *like* this way of coming to school."

"We can turn right around and go back home," Keller said. Iliana shut up.

Galen kept pace behind them, silent and focused. It was Nissa's usual position when the team wasn't heading for a car, and Keller couldn't help feeling the difference. She didn't *like* having someone behind her she couldn't trust absolutely. And although the enemies didn't seem to know yet that Galen was important, if they found out, he'd become a target.

Face it, she thought. This setup is a *disaster*, security-wise. This is a horrendous accident waiting to happen.

Her nerves were wound so tightly that she jumped at the slightest sound.

They shepherded Iliana to her locker, then up a staircase to the third floor. The halls were almost empty, which was exactly as Keller had planned it.

But of course that meant they were late for class.

Nissa slid in beside them just as they opened the door. They entered as a group, and the teacher stopped talking and looked at them. So did everybody else in the room.

Quite a few jaws dropped open.

Keller allowed herself a grim inner smile.

Yeah, they were probably a bit of a shock for a small town. Four Night People—well, former Night People, anyway. A witch who was almost as small as Iliana, with a mop of vivid strawberry blond curls and a face like a pixie on holiday. A vampire girl who looked like cool perfection straight out of a magazine, with cropped mink-colored hair and a strangely penetrating gaze. A shapeshifter boy who could have taken the place of any prince in a book of fairy tales, with hair like old gold and classically sculptured features.

And, of course, a panther. Which happened to be walking on two feet at the moment, in the guise of a tall girl with a tense, wary expression and black hair that swirled witchlike around her.

And, of course, there was Iliana in the midst of them, looking like a ballet dancer who had blundered in from the *Nutcracker Suite.*

There was a silence as the two groups stared at each other.

Then the teacher snapped shut his book and advanced on them. Keller held herself ready. He had a neatly trimmed beard and a dangerous expression.

It was Iliana who took him on, though. She stepped forward before Keller could draw a breath to speak.

"Mr. Wanamaker! These are my cousins! Well—some of them are my cousins. They're from . . . California. Hollywood! They're here to . . . do research for . . ."

"We're really just visiting," Keller cut in.

"A new show about a high school. Not like that *other* show. It's more of a reality-based—"

"It's just a visit," Keller said.

"But your dad *is* a famous producer," Iliana said. She added in an undertone to Mr. Wanamaker, "You know, like that other producer."

All eyes, including the teacher's, fixed on Keller.

"Yes—that's right," Keller said, and smiled while clenching her teeth. "But we're still just visiting." She nudged Winnie with her elbow, but it wasn't necessary. Winnie was already staring at the teacher, brainwashing him with witch power.

Mr. Wanamaker blinked. He weighed the book he was holding as if he were Hamlet holding Yorick's skull. He looked at it, then he looked at Winnie and blinked again.

Then he shrugged and looked at the ceiling. "Okay. Whatever. Sit down. There are some chairs at the back. And I'm still marking you tardy." But Keller noticed that as he returned to his desk, his posture was very erect.

She did the best she could to glare at Iliana without

drawing any further attention to them. "A famous producer?" she whispered through her teeth.

"I don't know. It was more interesting than just saying you're friends."

You don't need life to get any more interesting, Bubble-brain, Keller thought, but she didn't say anything.

She found one thing out that surprised her, though, and she found it out quickly. Her job was made harder by the fact that everyone at the school was in love with Iliana.

It was strange. Keller was used to getting attention from guys—and ignoring it. And Nissa and Winnie both were the type that had to beat them off with sticks. But here, although the guys looked at her and Nissa and Winnie, their eyes always seemed to return to Iliana.

At break, they crowded around her like bees around a flower. And not just guys, either. Girls, too. Everyone seemed to have something to say to her or just wanted to see her smile.

It was a bodyguard's nightmare.

What do they *see* in her? Keller thought, frustrated almost beyond endurance as she tried to edge Iliana away from the crowd. I mean, aside from the obvious. But if all this is about her looks . . .

It wasn't. It didn't seem to be. They weren't all hitting on her for dates.

"Hey, Iliana, my granddaddy loved that get well card you made."

"Illie, are you going to tie the ribbons this year for the

Christmas benefit bears? Nobody else can make those teeny-weeny bows."

"Oh, Iliana, something awful! Bugsy had five puppies, and Mom says we can't keep them. We've got to find them all homes."

"Iliana, I need help—"

"Wait, Iliana, I have to ask you—"

Okay, but why come to *her*? Keller thought as she finally managed to detach the girl from her fan club and steer her into the hall. I mean, she can hardly be the best problem solver in this school, can she?

There was one guy who seemed to like Iliana for the obvious. Keller disliked him on sight. He was good-looking in a carefully manicured way, with deep chestnut hair, deep blue eyes, and very white teeth. He was wearing expensive clothes, and he smiled a lot, but only at Iliana.

"Brett," Iliana said as he accosted them in the hall.

Brett Ashton-Hughes. One of the rich twins who were having the birthday party on Saturday night. Keller disliked him even more, especially when he gave her a coolly appreciative once-over before returning his attention to Iliana.

"Hey, blondie. You still coming Saturday?"

Iliana giggled. Keller stifled the urge to hit something.

"Of course, I'll be there. I wouldn't miss it."

"Because, you know, it would kill Jaime if you didn't come. We're only inviting a few people, and we'll have the whole west wing to ourselves. We can even dance in the ball-room."

Iliana's eyes went dreamy. "That sounds so romantic. I always wanted to dance in a real old-fashioned ballroom. I'll feel just like Scarlett O'Hara."

No, Keller thought. No, no, no. No *way* is she going there. She's going to the Solstice Ceremony, where the shape-shifters and the witches are meeting, even if I have to drag her by the hair.

She caught Nissa's eye and saw that Nissa was thinking the same. Galen and Winnie were simply watching Brett with troubled looks on their faces.

"Yeah, and I can be Brett Butler," Brett was saying. "Plus, the indoor swimming pool will be heated. So if you get tired of being Scarlett, you can be a mermaid for a while."

"It sounds wonderful! Tell Jaime I said so."

Winnie bit her lip. Keller got a fresh grip on Iliana's arm and started guiding her away.

"So it's a promise, right?" Brett called after her.

Keller *squeezed*.

"Yes, but—oh." Iliana managed to smile and wince at the same time, her arm limp in Keller's grasp, "Oh, Brett, there's one thing. I've got my cousin and her friends staying with me."

Brett hesitated an instant, giving each girl on Keller's team the appraising look. Then he shrugged and flashed a smile. "Hey, no problem. Bring them all. Your friends are our friends."

"That *wasn't* what I was trying to tell you," Keller said when they were away from Brett.

Iliana was rubbing her arm with an aggrieved expression. "Then what? I thought it would be fun for you to go."

"What do you mean, 'then what'? You're going to the Solstice Ceremony that night, so you shouldn't have promised him."

"I am *not* going to the Solstice Ceremony that night, because I'm not the one you're looking for."

It wasn't the time to argue. Keller kept her moving down the hall.

Keller wasn't happy. Her nerves were all prickling, and she felt like a cat with its fur standing on end.

Very soon, Iliana wasn't happy, either.

"I always eat lunch in the cafeteria!"

"Not today," Keller said, knowing she sounded as brusque and tired as she felt. "We can't risk it. You've got to be in a room, alone, someplace where we can control access to you."

"The music room," Winnie said helpfully. "I saw it on the map and asked a girl about it in English class. It's open during lunch, and there's only one door."

"I don't *want* to—"

"You don't have a choice!"

Iliana sulked in the music room. The problem was that she wasn't very good at sulking, and you could only tell she was doing it because when she offered her cookies to Nissa, she only insisted once.

Keller paced nervously in the hallway in front of the door. She could hear Winnie and Galen inside talking. Even Galen's *voice* sounded white-faced and strained.

Something's wrong . . . I've had a bad feeling ever since we got to this school . . . and it isn't any easier having *him* around.

Part of her was worried that he might take this opportunity to come and try to talk to her. And part of her, a very deep inside part, was furious because he wasn't doing it.

Goddess! I've got to get my mind clear. Every second that I'm not in control of my emotions means an opportunity for *them.*

She was so absorbed in yelling at herself that she almost missed the girl walking past her. Keller was almost at the end of the hall, and she had to do a double-take to realize that somebody had just calmly slipped by.

"Hey, wait," she said to the girl's back. The girl was medium-sized and had hair the soft brown of oak leaves, slightly longer than shoulder-length. She was walking fast.

She didn't stop.

"Wait! I'm talking to you, girl! That door is off-limits."

The girl didn't turn, didn't even pause. She was almost at the door to the music room.

"*Stop right there!* Or you're going to get hurt!"

Not even a hesitation in the girl's step. She turned into the door.

A thousand red alerts went off in Keller's head.

CHAPTER 9

Keller reacted instantly and instinctively.

She changed.

She did it on the leap this time. Rushing the process along, pushing it from behind. She wanted to be entirely a panther by the time she landed on the girl's back.

But some things can't be rushed. She felt herself begin to liquefy and flow . . . formlessness . . . pleasure . . . the utter freedom of not being bound to any single physical shape. Then re-formation, a stretching of all her cells as they reached to become something different, to unfurl like butterfly wings into a new kind of body.

Her jumpsuit misted into the fur that ran along her body, up and down from the stomach in front, straight down from the nape of her neck in back. Her ears surged and then firmed up, thin-skinned, rounded, and twitching already. From the base of her spine, her tail sprang free, its slightly clubbed end whipping eagerly.

That was how she landed.

She knocked the girl cleanly over, and they both went rolling on the floor. When they stopped, Keller was crouching on the girl's stomach.

She didn't want to kill the girl. She needed to find some things out first. What kind of Night Person the girl was, and who'd sent her.

The only problem was that now, as she knelt with her hands gripping the girl's arms, staring into dark blue eyes under soft brown bangs, she couldn't sense anything of the Night World in the girl's life energy.

Shapeshifters were the uncontested best at that. They could tell a human from a Night Person nine times out of ten. And this girl wasn't even in the "maybe" range. She was giving off purely human signals.

Not to mention screaming. Her mouth was wide open, and so were her eyes, and so were her pupils. Her skin had gone blue-white like someone about to faint. She looked utterly bewildered and horrified, and she wasn't making a move to fight back.

Keller's heart sank.

But if the girl was human and harmless, why hadn't she listened when Keller had shouted at her?

"Boss, we have to shut her *up*." It was Winnie, yelling

above the girl's throaty screams. As usual, Nissa didn't say a word, but she was the one who shut the music room door. By then, Keller had recovered enough to put a hand over the girl's mouth. The screaming stopped.

Then she looked at the others.

They were staring at her. Wide-eyed. Keller felt like a kitten with its paw in the canary cage.

Here she was, sitting on this human girl's midriff, in her half-and-half form. Her ears and tail were a panther's, and she was clothed from her snug boots to her shoulders in fur. It fit her like a black velvet jumpsuit, a sleeveless one that left her arms and neck bare. The hair on her head was still a human's and swirled around her to touch the floor on every side.

Her face was human, too, except for the pupils of her eyes, which were narrow ovals, reacting to every change of light and shadow. And her teeth. Her canines had become delicately pointed, giving her just the slightest hint of fangs.

She blinked at Galen, not sure what she saw in his expression. He was definitely staring at her, and there was *some* strong emotion pulling his face taut and making that white line around his mouth.

Horror? Disgust? He was a shapeshifter himself—or he would be if he could ever make up his mind. He'd seen her in panther form. Why should he be shocked at this?

The answer flashed back at Keller from some deep part of her brain. Only because I'm a monster this way. Panthers are part of nature and can't be blamed for what they do. I'm a savage thing that doesn't manage to be either an animal or a person.

And I'm dangerous in this form. Neither half of me is really in control.

Someone who's never changed could never understand that.

Galen took a step toward her. His jaw was tense, but his gold-green eyes were fixed on hers, and his hand was slightly lifted. Keller wondered if it was the gesture of a hostage negotiator. He opened his mouth to say something.

And Iliana came to life, jumping up and running past him and shrieking at Keller all at once.

"What are you *doing*? That's Jaime! What are you *doing* to her?"

"You know her?"

"That's Jaime Ashton-Hughes! She's Brett's *sister*! And she's one of my best *friends*! And you *attacked* her! Are you all *right*?"

It was all shrieked at approximately the same decibel level, but on the last sentence, Iliana looked down at Jaime.

Keller moved her palm from Jaime's mouth. As it turned out, though, that didn't seem to be necessary. Jaime raised her free hand and began to make swift, fluid gestures at Iliana with it.

Keller stared, and then her insides plummeted.

She let go of the girl's other arm, and the gestures immediately became two-handed.

Oh. Oh . . . darn.

Keller could feel her ears flatten backward. She looked unhappily at Iliana.

"Sign language?"

"She's got a hearing impairment!" Iliana glared at Keller, all the while making gestures back at Jaime. Her motions were awkward and stilted compared to Jaime's, but she clearly had some idea what she was doing.

"I didn't realize."

"What difference does it make how well she can hear?" Iliana yelled. "She's my friend! She's president of the senior class! She's chair for the Christmas Benefit bazaar! What did she do to you, ask you to buy a teddy bear?"

Keller sighed. Her tail was tucked up close to her body, almost between her legs, and her ears were flatter than ever. She climbed off Jaime, who immediately scooted backward and away from her, still talking rapidly with her hands to Iliana.

"The difference," Keller said, "is that she didn't stop when I told her to. I yelled at her, but . . . I didn't realize. Look, just tell her I'm sorry, will you?"

"*You* tell her! Don't talk about her as if she isn't here. Jaime can lip-read just fine if you bother to face her." Iliana turned to Jaime again. "*I'm* sorry. Please don't be mad. This is terrible—and I don't know how to explain. Can you breathe now?"

Jaime nodded slowly. Her dark blue eyes slid to Keller, then back to Iliana. She spoke in a hushed voice. Although it was flat in tone and some of the sounds were indistinct, it was actually rather pleasant. And the words were perfectly understandable.

"What . . . is it?" she asked Iliana. Meaning Keller.

But then, before Iliana could answer, Jaime caught herself. She bit her lip, looked at the floor for a moment, then braced herself and looked at Keller again. She was frightened, her body was shrinking, but this time her eyes met Keller's directly.

"What . . . are you?"

Keller opened her mouth and shut it again.

A hand closed on her shoulder. It was warm, and it exerted brief pressure for an instant. Then it pulled away, maybe as if revolted because it was resting on fur.

"She's a person," Galen said, kneeling down beside Jaime. "She may look a little different right now, but she's as much of a person as you are. And you have to believe that she didn't mean to hurt you. She made a mistake. She thought you were an enemy, and she reacted."

"An enemy?" There was something about Galen. Jaime had relaxed almost as soon as he got down on her level. Now she was talking to him freely, her hands flying gracefully as she spoke aloud, emphasizing her words. Her face was pretty when it wasn't blue with suffocation, Keller noticed. "What are you talking about? What kind of enemy? Who *are* you people? I haven't seen you around school before."

"She thought—well, she thought you were going to hurt Iliana. There are some people who are trying to do that."

Jaime's face changed. "Hurt Iliana? Who? They'd better not even *try*!"

Winnie had been twitching throughout this. Now she muttered, "Boss . . ."

"It doesn't matter," Keller said quietly. "Nissa's going to have to blank her memory anyway." It was too bad, in a way, because this girl's reaction to the Night World was one of the most sensible Keller had ever seen. But it couldn't be helped.

Keller didn't look at Iliana as she spoke; she knew there was going to be an argument. But before it started, she had one final thing to say.

"Jaime?" She moved and got instant attention. "I'm sorry. Really. I'm sorry I frightened you. And I'm really sorry if I hurt you." She stood up, not waiting to see if she was forgiven. What difference did it make? What was done was already done, and what was about to happen was inevitable. She didn't *expect* to be forgiven, and she didn't care.

That was what she told herself, anyway.

Iliana did argue. Keller tried not to let Jaime see much of it, because that would only make her more scared and miserable, and the end really was inescapable. Leaving her memory intact would be dangerous not only for Iliana but for Jaime herself.

"It's death for a human to find out about the Night World," Keller said flatly. "And it's worse than death if the dragon and his friends think she's got any information about the Wild

Power. You don't want to know what they'll do to try and get it out of her, Iliana. I *promise* you don't."

And, finally, Iliana gave in, as Keller had known she would have to from the beginning. Nissa moved up behind Jaime like a whisper and a shadow and touched her on the side of her neck.

Although witches were the experts at brainwashing, at inserting new ideas and convictions, vampires were the best at wiping the slate clean. They didn't use spells. It was something they were born with, the power to put their victim into a trance and smooth away hours or even days of memory. Jaime looked into Nissa's silvery-brown eyes for maybe seventy seconds, and then her own blue eyes shut, and her body went limp. Galen caught her as she fell.

"She'll wake up in a few minutes. It's probably best if we leave her here and get out," Nissa said.

"Lunch is over, anyway," Keller said. In the quiet minutes while Jaime was being hypnotized, Keller had finally managed to convince her body that there was no danger. It was only then that she could relax enough to change back.

Her ears collapsed, her tail retracted. Her fur misted into jumpsuit and skin. She blinked twice, noticing the difference in brightness as her pupils changed, and the tips of her fangs melted into ordinary teeth.

She stood up, shifting her shoulders to get used to the human body again.

They were all subdued as they escorted Iliana back to classes. The quietest of all was Keller.

She had overreacted, let her animal senses throw her into a panic. It wasn't the first time in her life. The *first* time in her life had been when she was about three . . . but better not to think about that. Anyway, it wasn't even the first time in her career as an agent for Circle Daybreak.

An agent had to be ready for anything at any moment. Had to have radar running, in front, in back, and on all sides, all the time, and be prepared to react instinctively at the slightest stimulus. If that sometimes caused mistakes—well, it also saved lives.

And she wasn't sorry. If she had to do it over, she'd do it again. Better one nice brown-haired girl scared than Iliana hurt. Better, Keller thought with bleak defiance, one nice brown-haired girl *killed* than Iliana in the hands of the enemy. Iliana represented the future of the entire daylight world.

But . . .

Maybe she was getting too old for this kind of job. Or maybe too jumpy.

Iliana sat moodily during afternoon classes, like a fairy who'd lost her flower. Keller noticed Winnie and Nissa being extra vigilant—just in case their boss got preoccupied. She flashed them a sarcastic look.

"You waiting for me to slack off?" She poked Nissa in the ribs. "Don't hold your breath."

They smiled, knowing they'd been thanked.

And Galen . . .

Keller didn't want to think about Galen. He sat quietly but intently through each class, and she could tell his senses were expanded. He didn't try to speak to her, didn't even look at her. But Keller noticed that every so often he rubbed his palm against his jeans.

And she remembered the way his hand had pulled back from her shoulder. As if he'd touched something hot.

Or something repulsive . . .

Keller gritted her teeth and stared at various blackboards with dry and burning eyes.

When the last bell finally rang, she made the whole group wait in the chemistry classroom while the school emptied out. Iliana watched and silently steamed as her friends all left without her. Even the teacher packed up and disappeared.

"Can we go *now*?"

"No." Keller stood at the second-story window, looking down. All right, so I'm a tyrant, she thought. A nasty, unsympathetic, whip-wielding dictator who jumps on innocent girls and won't let people out of school. I like being that way.

Iliana wouldn't argue. She stood rigidly a few feet away, looking out the window herself but refusing to acknowledge Keller's presence.

Finally, Keller said, "All right. Nissa, get the car."

Galen said, "I'll do it."

The answer to *that*, of course, was, "No way." But Galen was going on.

"It's something useful I can do. I've been standing around all day, wishing I was trained at *something.* At least driving I can handle. And if anybody comes after me, I can run fast."

The answer to that was still no. But Keller couldn't bring herself to say it, because she couldn't bring herself to face him for a long debate. She was afraid of what she might see in the depths of those gold-green eyes.

It would be funny if she'd managed to turn the prince of the shapeshifters off from shapeshifting altogether. Wouldn't it?

"Go on," she said to Galen, still looking down onto the circular driveway in front of the school.

After he had gone, she said to Nissa, "Follow him."

That was how everyone happened to be where they were in the next few minutes.

Keller and Iliana were at the window, staring out at a cool gray sky. Winnie was at the door to the chemistry room, watching the hallway. Galen was a floor beneath them somewhere inside the school, and Nissa was a discreet distance behind him.

And standing beside the circular driveway, obviously waiting for a ride, was a girl with familiar brown hair. She was reading a book that didn't look like a textbook.

Jaime.

It all happened very fast, but there were still distinct stages of warning. Keller was aware of them all.

The first thing she noticed was a blue-green car that cruised down the street in front of the high school. It was going slowly, and she narrowed her eyes, trying to catch a glimpse of the driver.

She couldn't. The car passed on.

I should make her get away from the window, Keller thought. This wasn't as obvious a conclusion as it seemed. The Night People weren't in the habit of using sharpshooters to pick off their targets.

But it was still probably a good idea. Keller was tiredly opening her mouth to say it when something caught her attention.

The blue-green car was back. It was at the exit of the circular driveway, stopped but facing the wrong way, as if it were about to enter.

As Keller watched, it revved its engine.

Keller felt her hairs prickle.

But it didn't make any sense. Why on earth would Night People want to park there and draw attention to themselves? It had to be some human kids acting up.

Iliana was frowning. She had stopped tracing patterns in the dust on the windowsill. "Who's that? I don't know that car."

Alarms.

But still . . .

The car roared again and started moving. Coming the wrong way along the driveway.

And Jaime, right below them, didn't look up.

Iliana realized at the same time Keller did.

"Jaime!" She screamed it and pounded the window with one small fist. It didn't do the slightest good, of course.

Beside her, Keller stood frozen and furious.

The car was picking up speed, heading straight for Jaime.

There was nothing to do. Nothing. Keller could never get down there fast enough. It was all going to be over in a second.

But it was horrible. That giant metal thing, tons of steel, was going to hit about a hundred and ten pounds of human flesh.

"Jaime!" It was a scream torn from Iliana.

Below, Jaime finally looked up. But it was too late.

CHAPTER 10

The car coming. Iliana screaming. And the feeling of absolute helplessness—

Glass shattered.

Keller didn't understand at first. She thought that Iliana was trying to break the window and get Jaime's attention. But the window was safety glass, and what broke was the beaker in Iliana's hand.

Blood spurted, shockingly red and liquid.

And Iliana kept squeezing the broken glass in her hand, making more and more blood run.

Her small face was fixed and rigid, her lips slightly parted, her breath held, her whole expression one of complete concentration.

She was calling the blue fire.

Keller lost her own breath.

She's doing it! I'm going to see a Wild Power. Right here, right beside me, it's happening!

She wrenched her own gaze back to the car. She was going to see those tons of metal come to a stop just as the BART train on the video had. Or maybe Iliana would just deflect the car in its course, send it into the grassy island in the middle of the driveway.

In any case, she can hardly deny that she's the Wild Power now—

It was then that Keller realized the car wasn't stopping.

It wasn't working.

She heard Iliana make a desperate sound beside her. There was no time for anything more. The car was on top of Jaime, swinging up onto the curb.

Keller's heart lurched.

And something streaked out behind Jaime, hitting her from behind.

It knocked her flying toward the grassy island. Out of the path of the car.

Keller knew who it was even before her eyes could focus on the dark golden hair and long legs.

The car braked and screeched and swerved—but Keller couldn't tell if it had hit him. It went skidding, half on and half off the sidewalk. Then it corrected its course and roared along the driveway, speeding away.

Nissa came dashing out of the door below and stood for an instant, taking in the scene.

Above, Keller was still frozen. She and Iliana were both as motionless as statues.

Then Iliana made a little noise and whirled around. She was off and running before Keller could catch her.

She shot past Winnie, leaving a trail of flying red droplets.

"Come on!" Keller yelled.

They both went after her. But it was like chasing a sunbeam. Keller had had no idea the little thing could run like that.

They were right behind her all the way down the stairs and out the door. It was where Keller wanted to be, anyway.

There were two figures lying on the pavement. They were both very still.

Keller's heart was beating hard enough to break through her chest.

Amazing how, even after seeing so much in her life, she could still have the desperate impulse to shut her eyes. For the first moment, as her gaze raked over Galen's body, she wasn't sure if she could see blood or not. Everything was pulsing with dark spots, and her brain didn't seem able to put any kind of coherent picture together.

Then he moved. The stiff, wincing motion of somebody injured, but not injured badly. He lifted his head, pushed himself up on one elbow, and looked around.

Keller stared at him wordlessly. Then she made her voice obey her. "Did it hit you?"

"Just glanced off me." He got his legs under him. "I'm fine. But what about—"

They both looked at Jaime.

"Goddess!" Galen's voice was filled with horror. He scrambled up and took a limping step before falling to his knees.

Even Keller felt shock sweep over her before she realized what was going on.

At first glance, it looked like a tragedy. Iliana was holding Jaime, cradling her in her arms, and there was blood everywhere. All over the front of Iliana's sweater, all over Jaime's white shirt. It just showed up better on Jaime.

But it was Iliana's blood, still flowing from her cut hand. Jaime was blinking and lifting a hand to her forehead in bewilderment. Her color was good, and her breathing sounded clear if fast.

"That car—those people were crazy. They were going to hit me."

"I'm sorry," Iliana said. "I'm so sorry; I'm so sorry . . ."

She was so beautiful that Keller's heart seemed to stop.

Her fine skin seemed almost translucent in the cool afternoon light. That glorious hair was rippling in the wind behind her, every single strand light as air and moving independently. And her expression . . .

She was bending over Jaime so tenderly, tears falling like

diamonds. Her grief—it was *complete*, Keller thought. As if Jaime were her own dearest sister. She cared in a way that went beyond sympathy and beyond compassion and into something like perfect love.

It . . . transformed her. She wasn't a light-minded child anymore. She was almost . . . angelic.

All at once, Keller understood why everybody at school brought their problems to this girl. It was because of that caring, that love. Iliana didn't help them to make herself popular. She helped because her heart was open, without shields, without the normal barriers that separated people from one another.

And she was as brave as a little lion. She hadn't even hesitated when she saw Jaime in danger. She was afraid of blood, but she'd cut herself instantly, even recklessly, trying to help.

That was courage, Keller thought. Not doing something without being afraid, but doing something even though you *were* afraid.

In that moment, all of Keller's resentment of Iliana melted away. All her anger and exasperation and contempt. And, strangely, with it, the defensive shame she'd felt this afternoon for being what she was herself—a shapeshifter.

It didn't make sense. There was no connection. But there it was.

The flat but strangely pleasant voice of Jaime was going on. "I'm okay—it was just a shock. Stop crying now. Somebody pushed me out of the way."

Iliana looked up at Galen.

She was still crying, and her eyes were the color of violet crystal. Galen was kneeling on one knee, looking down worriedly at Jaime.

Their eyes met, and they both went still. Except for the wind ruffling Iliana's hair, they might have been a painting. A scene from one of the Old Masters, Keller thought. The boy with dark golden hair and that perfectly sculptured face, looking down with protective concern. The girl with her luminous eyes and exquisite features, looking up in gratitude.

It was a sweet and lovely picture. It was also the exact moment that Iliana fell in love with Galen.

And Keller knew it.

She knew before Iliana knew herself. She saw a sort of plaintive shimmer in Iliana's eyes, like more tears about to fall. And then she saw the change in Iliana's face.

The gratitude became something different, something more like . . . recognition. It was as if Iliana were discovering Galen all at once, seeing everything in him that Keller had been slowly learning to see.

They're both . . .

Keller wanted to think *idiots*, but the word wouldn't come. All she ended up with was *the same.*

Both of them. Idealists. Openhearted. Trying to rescue everyone.

They're perfect for each other.

"You saved her life," Iliana whispered. "But you could have been killed yourself."

"It just happened," Galen said. "I moved without thinking. But you—you're really bleeding . . ."

Iliana looked soberly down at her hand. It was the only thing that marred the picture; it was gory and shocking. But Iliana's gaze wasn't frightened. Instead, she looked wise beyond her years and infinitely sad.

"I . . . couldn't help," she said.

Keller opened her mouth. But before she could say anything, Nissa appeared beside Iliana.

"Here," she said in her practical way, loosening the carefully knotted scarf at her throat. "Let me tie it up until we can see if you need stitches." She glanced up at Keller. "I got the license plate of the car."

Keller blinked and refocused. Her brain started ticking again.

"Both of you, go get the car," she said to Nissa and Winnie. "I'll finish that." She took Nissa's place by Iliana. "Are you really all right?" she asked Jaime, careful to face her directly. "I think we need to take all three of you to the hospital."

Part of her expected to see a flinching as the dark blue eyes under the soft brown bangs met hers. But, of course, there wasn't any. Nissa's memory blanking had been too good. Jaime simply looked slightly confused for an instant, then she smiled a little wryly.

"I'm really okay."

"Even so," Keller said.

There was a crowd gathering. Students and teachers were running from various corners of the building, coming to see what the noise was about. Keller realized that it had actually been only a couple of minutes since the car had gone roaring and screeching along the sidewalk.

A few minutes . . . but the world had changed. In several ways.

"Come on," she said, and helped Jaime up. She let Galen help Iliana.

And she felt strangely calm and peaceful.

Galen turned out to have several pulled muscles and lots of scrapes and bruises. Jaime had bruises and a dizzy headache and double vision, which got her actually admitted to the hospital—hardly surprising, considering how many times she'd been knocked down that day, Keller thought.

Iliana needed stitches. She submitted to them quietly, which only seemed to alarm her mother. Mrs. Dominick had been called from home to the hospital. She sat with the baby in her lap and listened to Keller try to explain how Iliana had gotten cut while standing at the chemistry room window.

"And when she saw the car almost hit Jaime, she was so startled that she just squeezed the beaker, and it broke."

Iliana's mother looked doubtful for a moment, but it

wasn't her nature to be suspicious. She nodded, accepting the story.

Jaime's parents had been called to the hospital, too, and both Galen and Jaime had to give statements to the police. Nissa flashed Keller a glance when the policewoman asked if anyone had noticed the car's license plate.

Keller nodded. She had already had Nissa call the number in to Circle Daybreak from a pay phone, but there was no reason not to have the police on the case, too. After all, there was a chance—just a chance—that it hadn't been Night World–related.

Not much of a chance, though. Circle Daybreak agents would follow Jaime and her family after this, watching from the shadows and ready to act if the Night World showed up again. It was a standard precaution.

Both Mr. and Ms. Ashton-Hughes, Jaime's parents, came down from Jaime's floor to speak to Galen in the emergency room.

"You saved our daughter," her mother said. "We don't know how to thank you."

Galen shook his head. "Really, it just happened. I mean, anybody would have done it."

Ms. Ashton-Hughes smiled slightly and shook her head in turn. Then she looked at Iliana.

"Jaime says she hopes your hand heals quickly. And she

wanted to know if you're still going to the birthday party on Saturday night."

"Oh—" For a moment, Iliana looked bewildered, as if she'd forgotten about the party. Then she brightened. "Yeah, tell her that I am. Is she still going?"

"I think so. The doctor said she can go home tomorrow, as long as she keeps quiet for a few days. And *she* said she wasn't going to miss it even if her head fell off."

Iliana smiled.

It was well into the evening by the time they all got home. Everyone was tired, even the baby—and Iliana was asleep.

Mr. Dominick came hurrying out of the house. He was a medium-sized man with dark hair and glasses, and he looked very anxious. He came round to the backseat as Iliana's mother filled him in on the situation.

But it was Galen who carried Iliana inside.

She didn't wake up. Hardly surprising. The doctor had given her something for the pain, and Keller knew that she hadn't had much sleep the night before. She lay in Galen's arms like a trusting child, her face turned against his shoulder.

They looked . . . very good together, Keller thought. They looked *right.*

Winnie and Nissa hurried upstairs and turned down Iliana's sheets. Galen gently lowered her to the bed.

He stood looking down at her. A strand of silvery-gold

hair had fallen across her face, and he carefully smoothed it back. That single gesture told Keller more than anything else could have.

He understands, she thought. It's like that moment when she looked at him and discovered all at once that he's brave and gentle and caring. He understands that she cut herself to try and save Jaime, and that people love her because she loves them so much first. And that she couldn't be petty or spiteful if she tried, and that she's probably never wished another person harm in her life.

He sees all that in her now.

Mrs. Dominick came in just then to help get Iliana undressed. Galen, of course, went out. Keller gestured for Winnie and Nissa to stay, and followed him.

This time, she was the one who said, "Can I talk with you?"

They slipped into the library again, and Keller shut the door. With everything that was going on in the house, she didn't think anyone would notice.

Then she faced him.

She hadn't bothered to turn on the lights. There was some illumination from the window but not much. It didn't really matter. Shapeshifter eyes were good in the dark, and Keller was just as glad he couldn't study her face.

She could see enough of his as he stood by the window.

The light picked up the edge of his golden head, and she could see that his expression was troubled and a little uncertain.

"Keller—" he began.

Keller held up a hand to cut him off. "Wait. Galen, first I want to tell you that you don't owe me an explanation." She took a breath. "Look, Galen, what happened this morning was a mistake. And I think we both realize that now."

"Keller . . ."

"I shouldn't have gotten so upset at you about it. But that's not the point. The point is that things have worked out."

He looked bleak suddenly. "Have they?"

"Yes," Keller said firmly. "And you don't need to try and pretend otherwise. You care about her. She cares about you. Are you going to try and deny that?"

Galen turned toward the window. He looked more than bleak now; he looked terribly depressed. "I do care about her," he said slowly. "I won't deny it. But—"

"But nothing! It's *good*, Galen. It's what was meant to be, and it's what we came here for. Right?"

He shifted miserably. "I guess so. But Keller—"

"And it may just possibly save the world," Keller said flatly.

There was a long silence. Galen's head was down.

"We've got a chance now," Keller said. "It should be easy to get her to come to the ceremony on Saturday—as long as we can make her forget about that ridiculous party. I'm not saying use her feelings against her. I'm just saying go with it. She should *want* to be promised to you."

Galen didn't say anything.

"And that's all. That's what I wanted to tell you. And also that if you're going to act stupid and guilty because of something that was . . . a few minutes of silliness, a mistake—well, then, I'm not going to talk to you ever again."

His head came up. "You think it was a mistake?"

"Yes. Absolutely."

In one motion, he turned around and took her by the shoulders. His fingers tightened, and he stared at her face as if he were trying to see her eyes.

"And that's what you *really* think?"

"Galen, will you please stop worrying about my feelings?" She shrugged out of his grip, still facing him squarely. "I'm fine. Things have worked out just the way they should. And that's all we ever need to say about it."

He let out a long breath and turned toward the window again. Keller couldn't tell if the sigh was relief or something else.

"Just make sure she comes to the ceremony. Not that it should be difficult," she said.

There was another silence. Keller tried to read his emotions through his stance and failed completely.

"Can you do that?" she prompted at last.

"Yes. I can do it. I can try."

And that was all he said. Keller turned to the door. Then she turned back.

"Thank you," she said softly. But what she really meant was *Goodbye,* and she knew he knew it.

For a long moment, she thought he wouldn't answer. At last, he said, "Thank *you*, Keller."

Keller didn't know what for, and she didn't want to think about it right now. She turned and slipped out of the room.

CHAPTER 11

"She's what?" Keller said, coming out of the bathroom, toweling her hair.

"She's sick," Winnie said. "Runny nose, little temperature. Looks like a cold. Her mom says she has to stay home from school."

Well, it looks like we're having a run of good luck, Keller thought. It would be much easier to protect her inside the house.

Winnie and Nissa had spent the night in Iliana's room, while Keller, who was supposed to be asleep on the sofa bed in the family room, wandered the house in between catnaps. She'd asked Galen to stay in the guest room, and he had done just that.

"We can have a quiet day," she said now to Winnie. "This is great—as long as she gets well for Saturday."

Winnie grimaced.

"What?"

"Um—you'd better go in and talk to her yourself."

"Why?"

"You'd just better go. She wants to talk to you."

Keller started toward Iliana's room. She said over her shoulder, "Check the wards."

"I know, Boss."

Iliana was sitting up in bed, wearing a frilly nightgown that actually seemed to have a ribbon woven into the lace at the neck. She looked fragile and beautiful, and there was a delicate flush on her cheeks from the fever.

"How're you feeling?" Keller said, making her voice gentle.

"Okay." Iliana modified it with a shrug that meant *fairly rotten.* "I just wanted to see you, you know, and say goodbye."

Keller blinked, still rubbing her hair with the towel. She wasn't crazy about water, especially not in her ears. "Say goodbye?"

"Before you go."

"What, you think I'm going to school for you?"

"No. Before you *go.*"

Keller stopped toweling and focused. "Iliana, what are you talking about?"

"I'm talking about you guys leaving. Because I'm not the Wild Power."

Keller sat down on the bed and said flatly, "What?"

Iliana's eyes were that hazy iris color again. She looked, in her own way, as annoyed as Keller felt. "Well, I thought that was obvious. I can't be the Wild Power. I don't have the blue fire—or whatever." She tacked the last words on.

"Iliana, don't play the dumb blonde with me right now, or I'll have to kill you."

Iliana just stared at her, picking at the coverlet with her fingers. "You guys made a mistake. I don't have any power, and I'm not the person you're looking for. Don't you think you ought to go out and look for the *real* Wild Power before the bad guys find her?"

"Iliana, just because you couldn't stop that car doesn't mean that you don't have power. It could just be that you don't know how to tap into it yet."

"It *could* be. You're admitting that you're not sure."

"Nobody can be absolutely sure. Not until you demonstrate it."

"And that's what I can't do. You probably think I didn't really try, Keller. But I did. I tried so hard." Iliana's eyes went distant with agonized memory. "I was standing there, looking down, and I suddenly thought, *I can do it!* I actually thought I felt the power, and that I knew how to use it. But then when I reached for it, there was nothing there. I tried so hard, and I wanted it to work so much . . ." Iliana's eyes filled, and there was a look on her face that struck Keller to the heart. Then she shook her head and looked back at Keller. "*It wasn't there.* I know that. I'm certain."

"It has to be there," Keller said. "Circle Daybreak has been investigating this ever since they found that prophecy. 'One from the hearth that still holds the spark.' They've tracked down all the other Harmans and checked them. It *has* to be you."

"Then maybe it's somebody you haven't found yet. Some other lost witch. But it's *not me.*"

She was completely adamant and genuinely convinced. Keller could see it in her eyes. She had managed to vault back into denial in a whole new way.

"So I know you'll be leaving," Iliana went on. "And, actually, I'll really miss you." She blinked away tears again. "I suppose you don't believe that."

"Oh, I believe it," Keller said tiredly, staring at an exquisite gold-and-white dresser across the room.

"I really like you guys. But I know what you're doing is important."

"Well, is it okay with you if we just hang around for a little while longer?" Keller asked heavily. "Just until we see the light and realize you're not the Wild Power?"

Iliana frowned. "Don't you think it's a waste of time?"

"Maybe. But I don't make those decisions. I'm just a grunt."

"Don't you *treat* me like a dumb blonde."

Keller opened her mouth, lifted her hands, then dropped them. What she wanted to say was, *How can I help it when you're determined to be such a nincompoop?* But that wasn't going to get them anywhere.

"Look, Iliana, I really do have to stay until I get orders to go, all right?" Keller said, looking at her. "So you're just going to have to bear with us for a little while longer."

She stood up, feeling as if a weight had fallen on her. They were back to square one.

Or maybe not quite.

"Besides, what about Galen?" she said, turning back at the door. "Do you want *him* to go?"

Iliana looked confused. Her cheeks got even pinker. "I don't . . . I mean . . ."

"If you're not the Wild Power, you're not the Witch Child," Keller went on ruthlessly. "And you know that Galen has to promise himself to the Witch Child."

Iliana was breathing quickly now. She gulped and stared at the window. She bit her lip.

She really is in love with him, Keller thought. *And she knows it.*

"Just something to keep in mind," she said, and went out the door.

"Did you get any info on the license plate?"

Nissa shook her head. "Not yet. They'll call us when they have anything. And a courier brought this."

She handed Keller a box. It was the size of a shirt box but very sturdy.

"The scrolls?"

"I think so. There are wards on it, so we have to get Winnie to open it."

They had a chance after breakfast. Mrs. Dominick took the baby and went out shopping. Keller didn't worry too much about her. Just as Jaime was now being watched by Circle Daybreak agents, any members of Iliana's family who left the safety of the wards would be followed for their own protection.

They sat around the kitchen table—except for Iliana, who refused to join them and sat in the family room in front of the TV. She had a box of tissues, and every few minutes she would apply one to her nose.

"Before you open that," Keller said to Winnie, "how are the wards around the house?"

"They're fine. Intact and strong. I don't think anybody's even tried to mess with them."

Galen said, "I wonder why."

Keller looked at him quickly. It was just what she had been wondering herself. "Maybe it has something to do with what happened yesterday. And that's the other thing I want to talk about. I want to hear everybody's opinions. Who was in that car—Night Person or human? Why did they try to run over Jaime? And what are we going to do about it?"

"You go first," Winnie said. "I think you had the best view of it."

"Well, I wasn't the only one," Keller said. "There was

someone else beside me." She looked toward the living room. Iliana made a show of ignoring her completely.

Keller turned back. "But anyway, simplest first. Let's say the car was from the Night World. They cruised down the street in front of the school once before coming back. It's perfectly possible that they saw Iliana standing at the window. Maybe they were trying to determine for sure that she was the Wild Power. If she'd stopped the car, they'd have had solid proof."

"On the other hand," Nissa said, "they must be pretty sure she's the Wild Power. After all, it's really beyond question." She was looking earnestly at Keller, but she spoke loudly enough for Iliana to hear everything distinctly.

Keller smiled with her eyes. "True. Okay, more ideas. Winnie."

"Uh—right." Winnie sat up straighter. "The car was from the Night World, and they weren't actually trying to run over Jaime. They were going to snatch her because they somehow knew she'd been with us, and they figured she might have some information they could use."

"Nice try," Keller said. "But you were over by the door. You didn't see the way that car was driving. No way they were planning to grab her."

"I agree," Galen said. "They were going too fast, and they were heading right for her. They meant to kill."

Winnie dropped her chin into her hands. "Oh, well, fine. It was just an idea."

"It brings up something interesting, though," Nissa said thoughtfully. "What if the car was from the Night World, and they knew Iliana was watching, but they *weren't* trying to get her to demonstrate her power? What if they were just trying to intimidate her? Show what they were capable of, by killing her friend right in front of her eyes? If they knew how close she and Jaime were—"

"How?" Keller interrupted—

"Lots of ways," Nissa said promptly. "If they haven't snooped around that high school and talked to other kids, their intelligence system is worse than I think. I'll go farther. If they don't know that Jaime was in that music room with *us* yesterday at lunch, they ought to turn in their spy badges."

"If that's true, then maybe it's even simpler than we think," Galen said. "The law says that any human who finds out about us has to die. Maybe the car was from the Night World, and they didn't know that Iliana was watching—or they didn't care. They thought Jaime knew the secret, and they just wanted to carry out a good, old-fashioned Night World execution."

"And maybe the car *wasn't* from the Night World!" Iliana yelled suddenly, jumping off the family room couch. She wasn't even pretending not to listen anymore, Keller noted. "Did any of you ever think of that? Maybe the car just belonged to some crazed juvenile delinquents and it's all a massive coincidence! Well? Did you think of that?" She stood with her hands on her hips, glaring at all of them. The effect was somewhat diluted because she was wearing a frilly nightgown with a flannel robe over it and slippers with teddy bear heads on them.

Keller stood up, too. She wanted to be patient and make the most of this opportunity. But she never seemed to have much control where Iliana was concerned.

"We've thought of it. Circle Daybreak is trying to check on it—whether the car's registered to a human or a Night Person. But you're asking for a lot of coincidence, aren't you? How often do people deliberately run each other over in this town? What are the chances that you just happened to be watching when one of them did it?"

She felt Galen nudge her ankle with his foot. With an effort, she shut up.

"Why don't you come over here and talk with us about it?" he said to Iliana in his gentle way. "Even if you're not the Wild Power, you're still involved. You know a lot about what's been going on, and you've got a good mind. We need all the help we can get."

Keller saw Winnie glance at him sharply when he said the bit about Iliana having a good mind. But she didn't say anything.

Iliana looked a little startled herself. But then she picked up the box of tissues and slowly came to the kitchen table.

"I don't think well when I'm sick," she said.

Keller sat down. She didn't want to undo what Galen had accomplished. "So where does that leave us?" she asked, and then answered her own question. "Nowhere, really. It could be any of those scenarios or none of them. We may need to wait for whatever Circle Daybreak comes up with."

Keller looked around the table grimly. "And that's *dangerous*," she said. "Assuming it was the Night World that sent that car, they're up to something that we don't understand. They could attack us at any moment, from any direction, and we can't anticipate them. I need for all of you to be on your guard. If anything suspicious happens, even the littlest thing, I want you to tell me."

"It still bothers me that they haven't even tried to get in here," Galen said. "No matter how strong the wards are, they should at least be *trying.*"

Keller nodded. She had an uneasy feeling in the pit of her stomach about that. "They may be laying some kind of a trap somewhere else, and they may be so confident that we'll fall into it that they can afford to wait."

"Or it could be that they know I'm not the one," Iliana chimed in sweetly. "And they're off kidnapping the real Wild Power while you guys are wasting your time here." She blew her nose.

Keller gritted her teeth and felt a pain in her jaw that was getting familiar. "Or it could be that we just don't understand dragons," she said, possibly with more force than was necessary.

She and Iliana locked stares.

"You guys, you guys," Winnie said nervously. "Um, maybe

it's time we opened this." She touched the box Circle Daybreak had sent.

Iliana's eyes shifted to it with something like involuntary interest. Keller could see why. The box had the mysterious allure of a Christmas present.

"Go ahead," she told Winnie.

It took a while. Winnie did witchy things with a bag of herbs and some talismans, while everyone watched intently and Iliana mopped her nose and sniffled.

At last, very carefully, Winnie lifted the top of the box off.

Everyone leaned forward.

Piled inside were dozens and dozens of pieces of parchment. Not entire scrolls but scraps of them, each encased in its own plastic sleeve. Keller recognized the writing—it was the old language of the shapeshifters. She'd learned it as a child, because Circle Daybreak wanted her to keep in touch with her heritage. But it had been a long time since she'd had to translate it.

Iliana sneezed and said almost reluctantly, "Cool pictures."

There were cool pictures. Most of the scraps had three or four tiny illustrations, and some of them had only pictures and no writing. The inks were red and purple and deep royal blue, with details in gold leaf.

Keller spread some of the plastic sleeves across the table.

"Okay, people. The idea is to find something that will show us how to fight the dragon, or at least something to tell us how he might attack. The truth is that we don't even know what he can do, except for the black energy he used on me."

"Um, I can't *read* this, you know," Iliana pointed out with excessive politeness.

"So look at the pictures," Keller said sweetly. "Try to find something where a dragon is fighting a person—or, even better, getting killed by one."

"How do I know which one's the dragon?" It was an amazingly good question. Keller blinked and looked at Galen.

"Well, actually, I don't know. I don't know if anybody knows how to tell a dragon from another Night Person."

"The one in the mall—Azhdeha—had opaque black eyes," Keller said. "You could tell when you looked into them. But I don't suppose that's going to show up on a parchment like this. Why don't you just look for something with dark energy around it?"

Iliana made a tiny noise that in someone less delicate would have been called a snort. But she took a pile of the scraps and began poring over them.

"Okay," Keller said. "Now, the rest of us—"

But she never got to finish. The phone on the kitchen wall shrilled. Everyone glanced up toward it, and Iliana started to stand, but there was no second ring. After a long moment of silence, it rang again—once.

"Circle Daybreak," Keller said. "Nissa, call them back."

Keller tried not to fidget as Nissa obeyed. It wasn't just that she was hoping against hope that there was useful information about the car. For some reason she couldn't define, that very first ring of the phone had made her feel unsettled.

The early warning system of the shapeshifters. It had saved her life before, by giving her a hint of danger. But for what was about to happen now, it was entirely useless.

"Nissa Johnson here. Code word: Angel Rescue," Nissa said, and Keller saw Iliana's eyebrows go up. "Yes, I'm listening. What?" Suddenly, her face changed. "What do you mean, am I sitting down?" Pause. "Look, Paulie, just tell me whatever—"

And then her face changed again, and she did something Keller had never seen Nissa do. She gasped and brought a quick hand up to her mouth.

"Oh, Goddess, no!"

Keller's heart was pounding, and there was a boulder of ice in her stomach. She found herself on her feet without any memory of standing.

Nissa's light brown eyes were distant, almost blank. Her other hand clutched the receiver. *"How?"* Then she shut her eyes. "Oh, no." And finally, very softly, "Goddess help us."

CHAPTER 12

They were all on their feet by now. Keller's early warning system was screaming hysterically.

"I can't stand it anymore," Iliana hissed. "What's going *on*?"

Just then, Nissa said in a quenched voice, "All right, we will. Yes. Bye." She carefully replaced the handset.

Then she turned very slowly to face the others.

Or not to face them exactly. She was looking down at the floor in an unfocused way that scared Keller to death.

"Well, what is it?" Keller growled.

Nissa opened her mouth and raised her eyes to look at Winnie. Then she looked down again.

"I'm sorry," she said. "Winnie, I don't know how to say this." She swallowed and then straightened, speaking formally. "The Crone of all the Witches is dead."

Winnie's eyes went huge, and her hands flew to her throat. "Grandma Harman!"

"Yes."

"But how?"

Nissa spoke carefully. "It happened yesterday in Las Vegas. She was outside her shop, right there on a city street, in broad daylight. She was attacked . . . by three shapeshifters."

Keller stood and listened to her pounding heart.

Winnie breathed, "No. That's not possible."

"A couple of wolves and a tiger. A real tiger, Keller, not any smaller cat. There were human witnesses who saw it. It's being reported as some bizarre escape from a private zoo."

Keller stood rigid. Control, control, she thought. We don't have time for grieving; we've got to figure out what this *means.*

But she couldn't help thinking about Grandma Harman's good old face. Not a beautiful face, not a young face, but a *good* one, with intelligence and humor in the keen gray eyes. A face with a thousand wrinkles—and a story to go with each one.

How would Circle Daybreak ever get along without her? The oldest witch in the world, the oldest Hearth-Woman.

Winnie put both hands to her face and began to cry.

The others stood silently. Keller didn't know what to do. She was so bad at these emotional things, but nobody else was stepping forward. Nissa was even less good at dealing with emotion, and right now her cool face was sympathetic and sad but distant. Iliana looked on the verge of tears herself, but uncertain; Galen was staring emptily across the room with something like despair.

Keller awkwardly put an arm around Winnie, "Come on, sit down. Do you want some tea? She wouldn't like you to cry."

All pretty stupid things to say. But Winnie buried her strawberry blond head against Keller's chest, sobbing.

"Why? Why did they kill her? It isn't *right.*"

Nissa shifted uneasily. "Paulie said something about that, too. He said we should turn on CNN."

Keller set her teeth. "Where's the remote?" she said, trying not to sound rough.

Iliana picked it up and punched in a channel.

An anchorwoman was speaking, but for a second Keller couldn't take in what she was saying. All she could see were the words on the screen: CNN SPECIAL REPORT: ANIMAL PANIC.

And the footage, rough video from somebody's camcorder. It showed an unbelievable scene. An ordinary city street, with skyscrapers in the background—and in the foreground ordinary-looking people all mixed up with . . . shapes.

Tawny shapes. About the same size she was in panther form, and sinuous. They were on top of people. Four of them . . . no, five.

Mountain lions.

They were killing the humans.

A woman was screaming, flailing at an animal that had

her arm in its mouth to the elbow. A man was trying to pull another lion off a little boy.

Then something with a white-tipped muzzle ran directly at the camera. It jumped. There was a gasping scream and for an instant a glimpse of a wide-open mouth filled with two-inch teeth. Then the video turned to static.

"—that was the scene at the La Brea tar pits in Los Angeles today. We now go to Ron Hennessy, live outside the Los Angeles Chamber of Commerce . . ."

Keller stood frozen, her fists clenched in helpless fury.

"It's happening everywhere," Nissa said quietly from behind her. "That's what Paulie said. Every major city in the U.S. is being attacked. A white rhino killed two people in Miami. In Chicago, a pack of timber wolves killed an armed police officer."

"Shapeshifters," Keller whispered.

"Yes. Killing humans openly. They may even be *trans-forming* openly. Paulie said that some people claimed to see those Chicago wolves change. She took a deep breath and spoke slowly. "Keller, the time of chaos at the end of the millennium . . . it's happening *now.* They can't cover this up with a 'private zoo' story. This is it—the beginning of the time when humans find out about the Night World."

Iliana looked bewildered. "But why would shapeshifters start attacking humans? And why would they kill Grandma Harman?"

Keller shook her head. She was rapidly approaching numbness. She glanced at Galen and saw that he felt exactly the same.

Then there was a choked sound beside her.

"That's the question—*why*," Winnie said in a thick voice. Usually, with her elfin features and mop of curls, she looked younger than her age. But right now, the skin on her face was drawn tight, and her birdlike bones made her look almost like an old woman.

She turned on Keller and Galen, and her eyes were burning.

"Not just why they're doing it, why they're being allowed to do it. Where's the First House while all this is going on? Why aren't they monitoring their own people? Is it because they agree with what's happening?"

The last words were snapped out with a viciousness that Keller had never heard in Winfrith before.

Galen opened his mouth, then he shook his head. "Winnie, I don't think—"

"You don't think! You don't *know*? What are your parents doing? Are you saying you don't know *that*?"

"Winnie—"

"They *killed* our oldest leader. Our wise woman. You know, some people would take that as a declaration of war."

Keller felt stricken and at the same time furious at her own helplessness. She was in charge here; she should be heading Winnie off.

But she was a shapeshifter like Galen. And along with the

ability to transform and the exquisitely tuned senses, they both shared something unique to their race.

The guilt of the shapeshifters.

The terrible guilt that went back to the ancient days and was part of the very fabric of Keller's mind. No shapeshifter could forget it or escape it, and nobody who *wasn't* a shapeshifter could ever understand.

The guilt was what held Galen standing there while Winnie yelled at him, and held Keller unable to interrupt.

Winnie was right in front of Galen now, her eyes blazing, her body crackling with latent energy like a small but fiery orange comet.

"Who woke that dragon up, anyway?" she demanded. "How do we know the shapeshifters aren't up to their old tricks? Maybe this time they're going to wipe the witches out completely—"

"Stop it!"

It was Iliana.

She planted herself in front of Winnie, small but earnest, a little ice maiden to combat the witch's fire. Her nose was pink and swollen, and she was still wearing those teddy bear slippers, but to Keller she somehow looked valiant and magnificent.

"Stop hurting each other," she said. "I don't understand any of this, but I know that you're not going to get anywhere if you fight. And I know you don't *want* to fight." All at once, she flung her arms around Winnie. "I know how you feel—it's so awful. I felt the same way when Grandma Mary died, my mom's mother. All I could think of was that it was just so unfair."

Winfrith hesitated, standing stiffly in Iliana's embrace. Then, slowly, she lifted her own arms to hold Iliana back.

"We *need* her," she whispered.

"I know. And you feel mad at the people who killed her. But it's not Galen's fault. Galen would never hurt anybody."

It was said with absolute conviction. Iliana wasn't even looking at Galen. She was stating a fact that she felt was common knowledge. But at the same time, now that she was off her guard, her expression was tender and almost shining.

Yes, that's love, all right, Keller thought. And it's *good.*

Very slowly, Winnie said, "I know *Galen* wouldn't. But the shapeshifters—"

"Maybe," Galen said, "we should talk about that." If Winnie's face was pinched, his was set in steel. His eyes were so dark that Keller couldn't distinguish the color.

"Maybe we should talk about the shapeshifters," he said. He nodded toward the kitchen table, which was still strewn with the parchments. "About their history and about the dragons." He looked at Iliana. "If there's any chance of—of a promise ceremony between us, it's stuff you ought to know."

Iliana looked startled.

"He's right," Nissa said in her calm voice. "After all, that's what we were doing to start with. It's all tied together."

Keller's whole body was tight. This was something that she very much didn't want to talk about. But she refused to give in to her own weakness. With a tremendous effort, she managed to say steadily, "All right. The whole story."

"It started back in the days humans were still living in caves," Galen said when they were all sitting down at the kitchen table again. His voice was so bleak and controlled that it didn't even sound like Galen.

"The shapeshifters ruled then, and they were brutal. In some places, they were just the totem spirits who demanded human sacrifice, but in others . . ." He searched through the parchments, selected one. "This is a picture of a breeding pen, with humans in it. They treated humans exactly the way humans treat cattle, breeding them for their hearts and livers. And the more human flesh they ate, the stronger they got."

Iliana looked down at the parchment scrap, and her hand abruptly clenched on a tissue. Winnie listened silently, her pointed face stern.

"They were stronger than anyone," Galen said. "Humans were like flies to them. The witches were more trouble, but the dragons could beat them."

Iliana looked up. "What about the vampires?"

"There weren't any yet," Galen said quietly. "The first one was Maya Hearth-Woman, the sister of Hellewise Hearth-Woman. She made herself into a vampire when she was looking for immortality. But the dragons were naturally immortal, and they were the undisputed rulers of the planet. And they had about as much pity for others as a *T. rex* has."

"But *all* the shapeshifters weren't like that, were they?" Iliana asked. "There were other kinds besides the dragons, right?"

"They were all bad," Keller said simply. "My ancestors—the big felines—were pretty awful. But the bears and the wolves did their share."

"But you're right, the dragons were the worst," Galen said to Iliana. "And that's who *my* family is descended from. My last name, Drache, means 'dragon.' Of course, it was the *weakest* of the dragons that was my ancestor. The one the witches left awake because she was so young." He turned to Winnie. "Maybe you'd better tell that part. The witches know their own history best."

Still looking severe, Winnie thumbed through the parchment scraps until she found one. "Here," she said. "It's a picture of the gathering of the witches. Hecate Witch-Queen organized it. She was Hellewise's mother. She got all the witches together, and they went after the shapeshifters. There was a big fight. A really big fight."

Winnie selected another piece of scroll and pushed it toward Iliana.

Iliana gasped.

The parchment piece she was looking down at was almost solid red.

"It's fire," she said. "It looks like—it looks like the whole world's on fire."

Galen's voice was flat. "*That's* what the dragons did. Geological records show that volcanoes all over the world erupted around then. The dragons did that. I don't know how; the magic's lost. But they figured that if they couldn't have the world, nobody else would, either."

"They tried to destroy the world," Keller said. "And the rest of the shapeshifters helped."

"It almost worked, too," Winnie said. "But the gathering of witches managed to win, and they buried all the dragons alive. I mean, they put them to *sleep* first, but then they buried them in the deepest places of the earth." She bit her lip and looked at Galen. "Which probably wasn't very nice, either."

"What else could they do?" Galen said quietly. "They left the dragon princess alive—she was only three or four years old. They let her grow up, under their guidance. But the world was a scorched and barren place for a long time. And the shapeshifters have always been . . . the lowest of all the Night People."

"That's true," Nissa put in, her voice neither approving nor disapproving, simply making an observation. "Most Night People consider shapeshifters second-class citizens. They try to keep them down. I think, underneath, that they're still afraid of them."

"And there's never been an alliance between the shapeshifters and the witches," Keller said. She looked directly at

Iliana. "That's why the promise ceremony is so important. If the shapeshifters don't side with the witches, they're going to go with the vampires—"

She stopped abruptly and looked at Galen.

He nodded. "I was thinking the same thing."

"Those animal attacks," Keller said slowly. "It sounds as if the shapeshifters are already making their decision. They're helping to bring about the time of chaos at the end of the millennium. They're letting the whole world know that they're siding with the vampires."

There was a shocked silence.

"But how can *they* decide?" Winnie began.

"That's just it," Nissa said. "The question is, is it just the ordinary shapeshifters who're doing it, or is it official? In other words, has the First House already decided?"

Everyone looked at Galen.

"I don't think so," he said. "I don't think they'll make any decision yet, at least not in public. As for what they're doing in private, I don't know." His voice was still flat; it made no excuses.

He looked around the table, facing all of them. "My parents are warriors. They don't belong to Circle Daybreak, and they don't like the witches. But they don't like the vampires, either. More than anything, they'll want to be on whichever side is going to *win.* And that depends on which side gets the Wild Powers."

"I think they want something else," Keller said.

"Like?"

"They want to know that the witches are treating them fairly and not just trying to use them. I mean, if they thought that Circle Daybreak had found the Witch Child but wasn't going to promise her to their heir, well, they wouldn't be happy. It's not just a matter of having a kinship bond with the witches. It's a matter of feeling they're being treated as equals."

Nissa's light brown eyes narrowed, and she seemed almost to smile. "I think you've summed it up very well."

"So what it all comes down to," Keller said pointedly, "is what happens on Saturday night. If there's a promise ceremony, it means the witches have found the Wild Power and that they're willing to tie her to the shapeshifters. If not . . ."

She let the sentence trail off and looked at Iliana.

There, she thought. I've put it so plainly and simply, you can't deny it now. And you can't help but see what's at stake.

Iliana's eyes were like faraway violet storm clouds. Keller couldn't tell what she was thinking. Maybe that the situation couldn't be denied but that she herself wasn't involved.

Winnie took a deep breath. "Galen."

Her face was still drawn and unhappy, but the burning anger in her eyes was gone. She met Galen's gaze directly.

"I'm sorry," she said. "I shouldn't have said those things before. I know you're on our side. And I'm not like those people who don't trust the shapeshifters."

Galen smiled at her faintly, but his eyes were serious. "I

don't know. Maybe you shouldn't trust us. There are things in our blood—you can't get rid of the dragon completely."

It was strange. At that moment, his eyes looked not only dark but almost red to Keller. Exactly the opposite of their usual golden-green. It was as if a light were smoldering somewhere deep inside them.

Then Winnie abruptly extended her hand across the table. "I know *you*," she said. "And there's nothing bad in your blood. I won't mistrust you again."

Galen hesitated one instant, then reached out with something like gratitude and took her hand.

"Thanks," he whispered.

"Hey, if *I* were the Witch Child, I'd promise to you in a minute," Winnie said. Then she sniffled, but her smile was much more like the old Winnie's smile.

Keller glanced at Iliana almost casually and was riveted by what she saw.

The girl had changed again. Now she didn't look like a princess or an ice maiden but like a very young soldier about to go into battle. Or maybe a human sacrifice who could save her tribe by jumping into a volcano.

Her hair seemed to shine, silvery and pale, and her eyes were deep, deep violet in her small face. Her slight shoulders were back, and her chin was determined.

Slowly, staring at something invisible in the center of the table, Iliana stood up.

As soon as the motion drew their attention, the others fell quiet. It was obvious to everyone that something important was happening.

Iliana stood there, her hands clenched by her sides, her chest rising and falling with her breathing. Then she looked at Galen. Finally, she looked at Keller.

"I'm not the Witch Child any more than Winnie is. And I think you know that by now. But . . ." She took a breath, steadied herself.

Keller held her own breath.

"But if you want me to pretend to be, I'll do it. I'll go to the promise ceremony with Galen—I mean, if he'll do it with me." She gave a half-embarrassed glance at Galen, looking shy and almost apologetic.

"Will he ever!" Winnie said enthusiastically. Keller could have kissed her. Galen himself didn't rise to the occasion properly at all; instead he opened his mouth, looking uncertain.

Fortunately, Iliana was going on. "Then I'll go through with it. And maybe that will be enough for the shapeshifters to join with the witches, as long as they don't find out I'm a fake." She looked unhappy.

She was so adamant that for a moment Keller was shaken. Could it be she *wasn't* the Wild Power? But no. Keller *knew* she was. She just hasn't awakened her power yet. And if she continued to deny it, she never would.

She said, "Thank you, Iliana. You don't know how much,

how many lives you're going to save. Thank you."

Then the excitement got the better of her, and she took Iliana by the arm and gave her a sort of shaking squeeze of affection.

"You're a trooper!" Winnie said, and hugged her hard. "I knew you'd come through all the time, I really did."

Nissa smiled at her with genuine approval. Galen was smiling, too, although there was something in his eyes . . .

"There's just one thing," Iliana said a little bit breathlessly, rubbing her arm where Keller had gripped it. "I'll do this. I said I would. But I have two conditions."

CHAPTER 13

Keller's excitement deflated. "Conditions?"

"You can have anything you want," Winnie said, blinking away happy tears. "Cars, clothes, books . . ."

"No, no, I don't want *things*," Iliana said. "What I mean is, I'm doing this because I can't just stand around and *not* do anything when stuff like that is going on." She shivered. "I have to do anything I can to help. But. I'm still not the right person. So the first condition is that while I'm pretending to be the Wild Power, you guys have somebody out looking for the real one."

Keller said smoothly, "I'll tell Circle Daybreak. They'll keep looking and checking other Harmans. They'll do it for as long as you want them to."

They would, too. It was a small price to pay.

"And the other condition?" Keller asked.

"I want to go to Jaime's party on Saturday."

Instant uproar. Even Nissa was talking over people. Keller cut short her own exclamations and gestured for everybody to shut up.

Then she looked Iliana dead in the eye.

"It's impossible. And you *know* it's impossible. Unless you've found a way to be in two places at once."

"Don't be stupid," Iliana said. That small, determined chin was tight. "I mean *before* the promise ceremony thing. I want to go just for an hour or two. Because she's one of my very best friends, and she's gotten attacked twice because of me."

"So what? You're already making it up to her. You're saving her life and her twin brother's life and her parents' lives—"

"No, I'm *not.* I'm faking being a Wild Power when I know it isn't true. I'm acting a lie." There were tears in Iliana's eyes now. "But I'm not going to hurt Jaime's feelings, and I'm not going to break my promise to her. And that's that. So if you want me to go through with your little charade, I'll do it, but I want to go to the party first."

There was a silence.

Well, she's stubborn. I'll give her that, Keller thought. Once she decides on something, she absolutely won't be budged on it. I guess that will be helpful when the Wild Powers fight the darkness someday.

But right now, it was simply infuriating.

Keller drew a very long breath and said, "Okay."

Winnie and Nissa looked at her sharply. They hadn't

expected her to give in so fast, and they were undoubtedly wondering if their boss had some trick up her sleeve.

Unfortunately, Keller didn't. "We'll just have to work something out," she said to her team. "Make it as safe as possible, and stick by her every minute."

Winnie and Nissa exchanged unhappy glances. But they didn't say anything.

Keller looked at Iliana. "The one thing is, you *have* to be at the Solstice Ceremony at midnight. They're meeting in Charlotte, so that's about twenty minutes' drive, and we'd better leave plenty of time for safety. Say an hour at the least. If you're not there, where the shapeshifters and the witches are meeting, at exactly midnight—"

"My coach turns into a pumpkin," Iliana said tartly. She swabbed her nose with a tissue.

"No, the shapeshifters walk out, and any chance of an alliance is gone forever."

Iliana sobered, stared at the table. Then she met Keller's eyes. "I'll be there. I know it, and you know why? Because *you'll* get me there."

Keller stared at her, astonished. She heard Winnie give a short yelp of laughter and saw that Nissa was hiding a smile.

Then she felt a smile pulling up the corner of her own lip. "You're right; I will. Even if I have to drag you. Here, shake on it."

They did. And then Iliana turned to Galen.

She had been watching him out of the corner of her eye ever since she'd first started talking. And now she looked hesitant again.

"If there's anything—any reason I *shouldn't* do it . . ." She fumbled to a stop.

Keller kicked Galen's ankle *hard.*

He glanced up. He still didn't look like the Galen she knew. Talking about the dragons had done something to him, thrown a shadow across his face and turned his eyes inward. And Iliana's announcement hadn't lightened anything.

Keller stared at him intently, wishing she had telepathy. Don't you dare, she was thinking. What's *wrong* with you? If you mess this up, after all the work we've done and with so much at stake . . .

Then she realized something. Before, when he'd been telling the history of the dragons, Galen had looked brooding and a little scary. Now, he still looked brooding but unutterably sad. Heart-stricken—and full of such regret.

She could almost hear his voice in her head. *Keller, I'm sorry . . .*

Don't be an idiot, Keller thought, and maybe she wasn't telepathic, but she was certain that he could read her eyes. What have you got to be sorry for? Hurry up and do what you're supposed to do.

Her heart was pounding, but she kept her breathing tightly controlled. Nothing mattered but Circle Daybreak and the alliance. Nothing. To think of anything else at a time like this would be the height of selfishness.

And love is for the weak.

Galen dropped his eyes, almost as if he had lost a battle. Then he turned slowly from Keller to Iliana.

Who was standing with tears about to fall, hanging like diamonds on her lashes. Keller felt a twisting inside her chest.

But Galen, as always, was doing exactly the right thing. He took Iliana's hand gently and brought it to his cheek in a gesture of humility and simplicity. He could do that without stopping looking noble for a moment.

After all, he *was* a prince.

"I'd be very honored to go through the promise ceremony with you," he said, looking up at her. "If you can bring yourself to do it with me. You understand everything I was telling you before—about my family . . ."

Iliana blinked and breathed again. The tears had magically disappeared, leaving her eyes like violets freshly washed in rain. "I understand all that. It doesn't matter. It doesn't change anything about *you*, and you're still one of the best people I've ever met." She blinked again and smiled.

Nobody could have resisted it. Galen smiled back.

"Not nearly as good as you."

They stayed that way for a moment, looking at each other, holding hands—and glowing. They looked perfect together, silver and gold, a fairy-tale picture.

That's it. It's done. She'll have to go through the ceremony now, Keller thought. As long as we can keep her alive, we've recruited a Wild Power. Mission accomplished.

I'm really happy about this.

So why was there a heaviness in her chest that hurt each time she breathed?

It was late that afternoon when the second call came.

"Well, they found the driver of the car," Nissa said.

Keller looked up. They'd moved the box full of scrolls to Iliana's bedroom when Mrs. Dominick came back from shopping. Now they had them untidily spread out on the floor while Iliana lay on the bed heavy-eyed and almost asleep. She perked up when Nissa came in.

"Who was it?"

"A shapeshifter. Name of Fulton Arnold. He lives about ten miles from here."

Keller tensed. "Arnold. 'Eagle ruler.'" She glanced at Galen.

He nodded grimly. "The eagles are going to have some explaining to do. Damn it, they've always been hard to get along with, but this . . ."

"So it *was* connected with the Night World," Winnie said. "But did Circle Daybreak figure out why?"

Nissa sat down on the chair in front of Iliana's gold-and-white vanity. "Well, they've got an idea." She looked at Galen. "You're not going to like it."

He put down a piece of scroll and sat up very straight, bleak and self-contained. "What?"

"You know all our theories about why shapeshifters are attacking humans? Whether it's just the common 'shifter on the street or orders from the First House and so on? Well, Circle Daybreak thinks it's orders, but not from the First House."

"The shapeshifters wouldn't take orders from vampires," Galen said stiffly. "So the Night World Council is out."

"They think it's the dragon."

Keller shut her eyes and hit herself on the forehead.

Of course. Why hadn't she thought of it? The dragon giving direct orders, setting himself up as a legendary ruler who had returned to save the shapeshifters. "It's like King Arthur coming back," she muttered.

On her bed, Iliana was frowning in shock. "But you said dragons were evil. You said they were cruel and horrible and tried to destroy the world."

"Right," Keller said dryly. Only Iliana would think that this constituted a reason not to follow them. "They were all those things. But they were also strong. They kept the shapeshifters on top. I'm sure there are plenty of 'shifters who'd welcome a dragon back." She looked at Galen in growing concern as she figured it out. "They're going to think it means a new era for them, maybe even a return to shapeshifter rule. And if *that's* what they think, nothing the First House says is going to make any difference. Even the mice are going to rally round Azhdeha."

"You mean the promise ceremony is no good?" Iliana sat up. The interesting thing was that she didn't look particularly relieved—in fact, Keller thought, she looked positively dismayed.

"No, so don't even get that idea," Keller said shortly. "What it means is—" She stopped dead, realizing suddenly what it *did* mean. "What it means is . . ."

Galen said, "We have to kill the dragon."

Keller nodded. "Yeah. Not just fight it. We have to get rid of it. Make sure it's not around to give orders to anybody. It's the only way to keep the shapeshifters from being split."

Iliana looked down soberly at the snowstorm of paper that covered her floor. "Does any of that stuff tell you how to kill a dragon?"

Keller lifted a piece of parchment, dropped it. "So far, none of this stuff has told us *anything* useful."

"Yeah, but we haven't even looked through half of it," Winnie pointed out. "And since you and Galen are the only ones who can read the writing, the parts Nissa and I have gone through don't really count."

There was definitely a lot of work left. Keller stifled a sigh and said briskly, "Well, we don't need to worry about killing the dragon right now. If we can fight him off long enough to get through the promise ceremony, we can worry about destroying him afterward. Winnie, why don't you and Nissa start trying to figure out a way to protect Iliana at the party Saturday? And Galen and I can stay up tonight and read through these scrolls."

Winnie looked concerned. "Boss, you're trying to do too much. If you don't sleep sometime, you're going to start cracking up."

"I'll sleep on Sunday," Keller said firmly. "When it's all over."

Keller had meant that she and Galen could study the scrolls separately that night. But when everybody else headed for their bedrooms, he stayed in the family room with her and watched the eleven o'clock news. More animal attacks.

When it was over, Keller pulled out her pile of scroll fragments. It was her way of saying good night, and much easier than looking at him.

But he just said quietly, "I'll get my half," and brought them out.

Keller felt uncomfortable. It wasn't that she could find any fault with what he was doing. He was studying his pieces of scroll intently and letting her do the same.

But every now and then, he would look at her. She could feel his eyes on her, feel that they were serious and steady and that he was waiting for her to look up.

She never did.

And he never said anything. After a while, he would always go back to his parchments. They worked on and on in silence.

Still, Keller was aware of him. She couldn't help it. She was a panther; she could sense the heat of his body even three feet away. She could smell him, too, and he smelled good. Clean and a little bit like the soap he used, and even more like himself, which was something warm and golden and healthy. Like a puppy with a nice coat on a summer afternoon.

It was very, very distracting. Sometimes the words on the scrolls blurred in front of her eyes.

But worst of all, worse than feeling his heat or smelling his scent or knowing his eyes were on her, was something more subtle that she couldn't exactly define. A connection. A sense of tension between them that she could almost touch.

The air was buzzing with it. It lifted up the little hairs on Keller's arms. And no matter how she tried to will it away, it only seemed to grow and grow.

Somehow the silence made it worse, made it more profound. I have to say something, Keller thought. Something casual, to show that I'm not affected.

She stared at the scrolls, which she was beginning to hate. If only she could find something useful . . .

Then she saw it. Right there on the scroll she was studying.

"Galen. There's something here—in a copy of the oldest records about dragons. It's talking about what the dragons can *do*, what their powers are besides the dark energy."

She read from the scroll, hesitating on words that were less familiar to her. "'A dragon has only to touch an animal and it is able to assume that animal's form, know all that the animal knows, do all that the animal can do. There is no'—I think it says 'limit'—'on the number of shapes it can master. Therefore, it is a true shapeshifter and the only one worthy of the name.' I told you this stuff was old," she added. "I think the original was written by the dragons' press agent during the war."

"'No limit on the number of shapes it can master,'" Galen repeated with growing excitement. "That makes sense, you know. That's what the First House has inherited, only in a diluted form. Being able to pick whichever shape we want to become—but only the first time. After that, we're stuck with it, of course."

"Do you have to touch an animal to learn its shape?"

He nodded. "That's how we choose. But if a dragon can touch *anything* and assume its shape—and change over and over . . ." His voice trailed off.

"Yeah. It's going to be awfully difficult to spot them," Keller said. The tension in the air had been somewhat discharged by talking, and she felt a little calmer. At least she could talk without the words sticking in her throat.

But Galen wasn't helping. He leaned closer, peering down at her scroll. "I wonder if it says anything else, anything about how to identify . . . wait. Keller, look down here at the bottom."

To do it, she had to bend her head so that his hair brushed her cheek. "What?"

"Horns, something about horns," he muttered almost feverishly. "You're better at translating than I am. What's this word?"

"'Regardless'? No, it's more like 'no matter.'" She began to read. "'But no matter what form it takes, a dragon may always be known—'"

"'By its horns,'" he chimed in, reading with her.

They finished together, helping each other. "'A dragon has from one to three horns on its forehead, and in some rare cases four. These horns'"—both their voices rose—"'which are *the seat of its power* are most cruelly removed by the witches who capture them, to steal from them the power of changing.'"

They both stopped. They kept staring at the parchment for what seemed endless minutes to Keller. Galen was gripping her wrist so hard that it hurt.

Then he said softly, "That's it. That's the answer."

He looked up at her and gave her wrist a little shake. "*That's the answer.* Keller, we did it; we found it."

"Shh! You're going to wake up the whole house." But she was almost as shaky with excitement as he was. "Let me think. Yeah, that guy Azhdeha could have had horns. His hair was all messy, covering his forehead, and I remember thinking that was a little strange. The rest of him looked so neat."

"You see?" He laughed breathlessly, exultantly.

"Yes. But—well, do you have any idea how hard it would be to try and take off a dragon's horns?"

"No, and I don't care. Keller, stop it, stop trying to dampen this! The point is, we *found* it. We know something about dragons that can hurt them. We know how to fight!"

Keller couldn't help it. His exhilaration was infectious. All at once, all the bottled-up emotions inside her started to come out. She squeezed his arm back, half laughing and half crying.

"You did it," she said. "You found the part."

"It was on your scroll. You were just about to get there."

"You were the one who suggested we look at the scrolls in the first place."

"You were the one—" Suddenly, he broke off. He had been looking at her, laughing, their faces only inches apart as they congratulated each other in whispers. His eyes were like the woods in summertime, golden-green with darker green motes in them that seemed to shift in the light.

But now something like pain crossed his face. He was still looking at her, still gripping her arm, but his eyes went bleak.

"You're the one," he said quietly.

Keller had to brace herself. Then she said, "I don't know what you're talking about."

"Yes, you do."

He said it so simply, so flatly. There was almost no way to argue.

Keller found one. "Look, Galen, if this is about what happened in the library—"

"At least you're admitting that something happened now."

"—then I don't know what's wrong with you. We're both shapeshifters, and there was a minute when we sort of lost our objectivity. We're under a lot of stress. We had a moment of . . . physical attraction. It happens, when you do a job like this; you just can't take it seriously."

He was staring at her. "Is *that* what you've convinced yourself happened? 'A moment of physical attraction?'"

The truth was that Keller had almost convinced herself that nothing had happened—or convinced her mind, anyway.

"I told you," she said, and her voice was harsher than she'd heard it for a long time. "Love is for weak people. I'm not weak, and I don't plan to let anything *make* me weak. And, besides, what is your problem? You've already got a fiancée. Iliana's brave and kind and beautiful, and she's going to be very, very powerful. What more could you *want*?"

"You're right," Galen said. "She's all those things. And I respect her and admire her—I even love her. Who could help loving her? But I'm not *in* love with her. I'm—"

"Don't say it." Keller was angry now, which was good. It made her strong. "What kind of prince would put his personal happiness above the fate of his people? Above the fate of the whole freaking world, for that matter?"

"I don't!" he raged back. He was speaking softly, but it was still a rage, and he was a little bit frightening. His eyes blazed a deep and endless green. "I'm not saying I won't go through with the ceremony. All I'm saying is that it's you I love. You're my soulmate, Keller. And you know it."

Soulmate. The word hit Keller and ricocheted, clunking inside her as it made its way down. When it hit bottom, it settled into a little niche made especially for it, fitting exactly.

It was the word to describe what had really happened in the library. No stress-induced moment of physical attraction and no simple romantic flirtation, either. It was the soulmate principle.

She and Galen were soulmates.

And it didn't matter a bit, because they could never be together.

CHAPTER 14

Keller put her hands to her face. At first, she didn't recognize what was happening to her. Then she realized that she was crying.

She was shaking, Raksha Keller who wasn't afraid of anyone and who never let her heart be touched. She was making those ridiculous little noises that sounded like a six-week-old kitten. She was dripping tears through her fingers.

The worst thing was that she couldn't seem to make herself stop.

Then she felt Galen's arms around her, and she realized that he was crying, too.

He was better at it than she was. He seemed more used to it and didn't fight it as hard, which made him stronger. He was able to stroke her hair and even to get some words out.

"Keller, I'm sorry. Keller . . . can I call you Raksha?"

Keller shook her head furiously, spraying teardrops.

"I always think of you as Keller, anyway. It's just—you, somehow. I'm sorry about all of this. I didn't mean to make you cry. It would be better if you'd never met me . . ."

Keller found herself shaking her head again. And then, just as she had the last time, she felt her arms moving to hold him back. She pressed her face against the softness of his sweatshirt, trying to get enough control of herself to speak.

This was the problem with having walls so hard and high and unscalable, she supposed. When they came down, they crumbled completely, shattering into nothingness. She felt utterly defenseless right now.

Unguarded . . . vulnerable . . . but not alone. She could feel more than Galen's physical presence. She could feel his spirit, and she was being pulled toward it. They were falling together, falling *into* each other, as they had in the library. Closer and closer . . .

Contact.

She felt the touch of his mind, and once again her heart almost exploded.

You're the one. You're my soulmate, his mental voice said, as if this were an entirely new idea, and he was just discovering it and rejoicing in it.

Keller reached for denial, but it simply wasn't around. And she couldn't pretend to someone who shared her thoughts.

Yes.

When I first saw you, he said, *I was so fascinated by you. I already told you this, didn't I? It made me proud to be a shape-shifter for the first time. Aren't you proud?*

Keller was disconcerted. She still wasn't finished crying—but, yes, she was. With his warmth and passion shining into her, his arms locked around her, his mind open to her . . . it was hard not to get swept up in it.

I guess I'm proud, she thought to him slowly. *But only of some parts of it. Other things . . .*

What things? he demanded, almost fiercely protective. *Our history? The dragons?*

No. Stuff you wouldn't understand. Things about—animal nature. Even now, Keller was afraid of letting him see some parts of her. *Leave it alone, Galen.*

All he said was, *Tell me.*

No. It happened a long time ago, when I was three. Just be glad you get to pick *what kind of animal you'll become.*

Keller, he said. *Please.*

You don't like animal nature, she told him. *Remember how you pulled your hand away when you touched my shoulder in the music room?*

In the . . . ? His mental voice trailed off, and Keller waited grimly to feel the memory of disgust in him. But what came wasn't revulsion. Instead, it was a strong sense of longing that he was somehow trying to smother. And choked, wry laughter.

Keller, I didn't pull away because I didn't like your fur. I did it because . . . He hesitated, then burst out, sounding embarrassed, *I wanted to pet you!*

Pet . . . ?

Your fur was so soft, and it felt so good when I moved my palm the wrong way against it—just like velvet. And—I wanted to—to do this. He ran a hand up and down her back. *I couldn't help it. But I knew it wasn't exactly appropriate, and you would probably break my jaw if I tried it. So I took my hand away.* He finished, still embarrassed, but half laughing. *Now, you tell me what you're not proud of.*

Keller felt very warm, and she was sure her face was flushed. It was just as well that it was hidden. It was too bad—there was probably never going to be a time to tell him that she wouldn't mind being petted like that . . .

I'm a cat, after all, she thought, and was distantly surprised to hear him chuckle. There were no secrets in this kind of soul-link, she realized, slightly flustered. To cover her embarrassment, she spoke out loud.

"The thing I'm not proud of—it happened when I was living with my first Circle Daybreak family. I used to spend a lot of time in my half-and-half form. It was easy for me to get stuck that way, and they didn't mind."

I wouldn't, either, Galen said. *You're beautiful like that.*

"Anyway, I was sitting on my foster mother's lap while she was combing my hair, and I don't know what happened, but something startled me. Some loud noise outside, maybe a car backfiring. I jumped straight up and tried to race for my hiding place under the desk."

Keller paused, made herself take an even breath. She felt Galen's arms tighten around her.

"And then—well, my foster mother tried to hold on to me, to keep me from being frightened. But all I could think of was danger, danger. So I lashed out at her. I used my claws—I have retractable claws in that form. I would have done anything to get away."

She paused again. It was so hard to tell this.

"She had to go to the hospital. I forget how many stitches she needed in her face. But I remember everything else—being taken to another foster family because that one couldn't handle me. I didn't blame them for sending me away, but I always wished I could have told her how sorry I was."

There was a silence. Keller could feel Galen breathing, and that gave her an odd sense of comfort.

Then he said quietly, out loud, "That's all?"

Keller started, then lifted her head a little and made herself answer the same way. "Isn't it enough?"

"Keller . . . you were just a baby. You didn't mean to do any harm; it was an accident. You can't blame yourself."

"I do blame myself. If I hadn't been taken over by my instinct—"

"That's ridiculous. Human babies do stupid things all the time. What if a human three-year-old falls into a swimming pool and somebody drowns trying to rescue her? Would you blame the baby?"

Keller hesitated, then rested her head on his shoulder again. "Don't be silly."

"Then how can you blame yourself for something you couldn't help?"

Keller didn't answer, but she felt as if a crushing load was sliding slowly off her. He didn't blame her. Maybe she wasn't to blame. She would always be sorry, but maybe she didn't need to be so ashamed.

She tightened her own arms around him. *Thank you,* she thought.

Oh, Keller. You're so wonderful, and you're so set against admitting it. Everything you do . . . shines.

Keller couldn't form any words for a moment. Then she said, *Galen? When you do choose a form, choose something gentle.*

I thought you thought everybody has to be a fighter, he said, and his mental voice was very quiet.

Some people shouldn't have to be.

Then she just let him hold her.

Another endless time, while they both seemed to be floating in soft, gold fire. It flared around them and through them, joining them. Sometimes she could hardly tell which thoughts were his and which were hers.

He said, *I used to write poetry, you know. Or try. My parents hated it; they were so embarrassed. Instead of learning to be a good hunter, their son was writing gibberish.*

She said, *There's this terrible dream I have, where I look out at the ocean and see a wall of water hundreds of feet high, and I know it's coming and I can never get away in time. Cats and water, you know. I guess that's why.*

He said, *I used to daydream about what kind of animal it would be most fun to be. But it always came down to the same thing, some kind of bird. You just can't beat flying.*

She said, *One thing I always had to hide from my foster mothers was how much I liked to shred things. I thought I was being so clever when I would hide their panty hose after I used my claws on them. But when I did it on the sheer curtains one day, everybody knew.*

They talked and talked. And Keller gave herself up to it, to the simple pleasure of his closeness and the feeling that for once she didn't have to hide or pretend or defend herself. It was such a blessed relief not to have to pretend at all.

Galen knew her, and he accepted her. All of her. He loved her self, not her black swirling hair or her long legs or the curve of her lips. He might admire those things, but he loved *her*, what she was inside.

And he loved her with a sweetness and a power that shook Keller to her soul.

She wanted to stay like this forever.

There was something else waiting for them, though.

Something she didn't want to think about but that loomed just outside the brightness and warmth that surrounded them.

The world . . . there's still a world out there. And it's in trouble.

And we can't ignore that.

Galen.

I know.

Very slowly, very reluctantly, Galen straightened, putting her away from him. He couldn't seem to let go of her shoulders, though. They sat that way, their eyes locked.

And the strange thing was that the mental connection wasn't broken. They could still hear each other as they held each other's gaze.

We can never be like this again, Keller said.

I know. He had faced it as clearly as she had, she realized.

We can't talk about it; we can't even be alone together. It isn't fair to Iliana. And we have to try to forget each other and just go on.

I know, he said for the third time. And just when Keller was marveling at his quiet acceptance, she saw tears in his gem-colored eyes. *Keller, it's my fault. If I weren't the son of the First House . . .*

We'd never have met. And that would have been worse.

"Would it?" he said out loud, as if he needed reassurance.

Yes. She gave the answer mentally, so that he could feel the truth of it. *Oh, Galen, I'm so glad we met. I'm so glad to have known you. And if we live through this, I'll be glad all my life.*

He took her into his arms again.

"We have it, Boss," Winnie said.

Her eyes were sparkling. Beside her, Nissa looked calmly enthusiastic.

"What?" Keller asked. She herself felt calmly alert, in spite of almost no sleep the night before. She and Galen had stayed up late, reading over the scrolls, making sure that there was nothing they had missed. They had already explained what they'd found to the others.

Now Winnie was grinning at her.

"How to protect Iliana at the party on Saturday. We've got it, and it's foolproof!"

Nothing is foolproof, Keller thought. She said, "Go on."

"It's like this. We put wards all around the Ashton-Hughes house, just like the wards Grandma Harman made for this house. The strongest possible from Circle Daybreak. But we put them around the house *now*, as soon as we can. We key them so that only humans can get in."

"And we add another layer of protection," Nissa said. "Circle Daybreak agents posted around the house, starting now. Nothing gets in, nothing gets out that they don't know about. That way, when we go to the party on Saturday, we know it's safe."

"We just *whisk* her from one safe place to another," Winnie said. "As long as we can keep her in here until Saturday night, there's no chance of any danger."

Keller considered. "We have to make sure the limo is safe, too. Absolutely safe."

"Of course," Winnie said. "I'll take care of it."

"And I'd want agents to check the people who go in somehow. Not just monitor. Would there be any way to do that?"

"Without the family knowing?" Nissa chewed her lip gently. "What if we set up some sort of road crew near the front gate? There's bound to be a gate; this is a mansion, right?"

"Check it out. And we'd better get plans of the house, too. I want us all to know the place by heart before we get there."

"City planner's office," Nissa said. "No, more likely the local historical society. The house is probably a historic monument. I'm on it."

Keller nodded. "Hmm." She tried to think if there was anything else to worry about. "Hmm, it sounds . . ."

They watched her, breath held.

"It sounds *good*," Keller said. "I think there's just the tiniest, slightest possibility that it might actually work. But I'm probably being overoptimistic."

Winnie grinned and socked her on the shoulder. "You, Boss? Perish the thought."

• • •

"It's so difficult," Iliana said. "I mean, what can you wear to both a birthday party and a promise ceremony?"

"And a Solstice Ceremony," Winnie said. "Don't forget that."

"You're trying to make things worse, aren't you?" Iliana held up one dress, then another. "What's right for a Solstice Ceremony?"

"Something white," Winnie suggested.

"That would be good for a promise ceremony, too," Keller said. She was doing her very best to be patient, and finding it easier than she had expected.

The last three days had been very quiet. Iliana had agreed to stay home from school even when her cold got better. Galen and Keller had scarcely spoken in that time, and they had never been alone.

And that was . . . all right. There was a quietness inside her to match the quiet air outside.

They both had jobs to do. And they would do them as well as possible. Keller just prayed that what they did would be enough.

"White? I don't know if I've got anything white. It has to be fancy because everything at Jaime's is fancy. I hope she's really okay."

"She's fine," Keller said. "You talked to her an hour ago." To her own relief, Jaime had stayed quietly at home for the past three days, too. The last thing Keller wanted was for that girl to be attacked again.

But the Ashton-Hughes house, at least, was safe. For three days, it had been buttoned up tight, with Circle Daybreak agents watching every person who went through the gates. And checking them, using the same wards that protected the house. No Night Person could cross the invisible line that encircled the grounds, and no person who tried to cross and was turned back by the wards would be allowed to leave without being tracked.

All we have to do is keep her safe during the drive, Keller thought. First to the mansion, then to the meeting place in Charlotte. We can do that. I know we can do that.

She checked her watch.

"Come on, kid, it's after eight," she said. "We should be moving soon."

Iliana and Winnie were both ransacking the closet.

"Pale blue," Winnie said, "pale lavender, pale pink . . ."

"It has to be *white*," Iliana said.

"I'm sorry I mentioned it."

A knock sounded on the door, and Nissa looked in. "We're back. You guys ready?"

"In a minute," Keller said. "How're things at the mansion?"

"Perfect. The witches say the wards are strong."

"Who's come in?"

"Caterers and a college band. That's all so far. All one hundred percent human according to the wards—and to Galen, who kept running up to the cars at the gate and trying to sell them Christmas Benefit teddy bears."

Keller almost grinned. Galen would be good at that. "The family must have thought he was crazy."

"They never came out and complained. Nobody's come out, in fact, which makes things easy on the surveillance team." She sobered. "Boss, why do you think the dragon hasn't tried something yet? He's cutting it awfully close."

"I don't know. I think . . ."

"What?"

"I think he must be betting it all on one throw of the dice. One all-out attack, fast and decisive."

"At the party."

"At the party," Keller said. "So we'd better be on our toes."

"We've got him locked out, though. Those wards are secure."

"I hope so."

From the closet, Iliana squealed, "I found it!"

She was holding a dress almost the color of her own hair, white with some sort of sparkling thread woven in. It draped in soft folds across her hip as she held it up for Winnie's inspection.

"Perfect," Winnie said. "You can get engaged in that dress; you can go to a birthday party; you can celebrate the Solstice—you can probably get *married* in it if you want."

"You can do whatever you want, but you have to do it now," Keller said, checking her watch again.

"But do you like it? I think I bought it last year."

"It's beautiful," Keller said, and then, as she saw the hurt in Iliana's violet eyes: "Really. It's beautiful. You'll look wonderful in it, and Galen will be—very impressed."

Where had that sudden hitch in her breath come from? She had gotten over it quickly, but she noticed that Iliana gave her an odd look.

"Now, come on, everybody," Keller said briskly, looking at Winnie and Nissa. "Are you two ready?"

They both looked down at their ordinary outfits, then looked back up and shrugged in chorus.

"Yeah."

"I guess they can think we're the help," Keller said. "Everybody check your transmitters. I want to be in constant contact once we get there."

"Right, Boss."

"Got it, Boss."

Iliana had put on the dress and was looking in the mirror. "My hair," she began, and then she glanced at Keller. "I'll just leave it down," she said. "Okay?"

"Down is fine, down is great." Keller glanced at her watch and tightened her belt.

"Down is just right for a Solstice Ceremony," Winnie said. She added in an undertone as Iliana started for the door, "Don't mind her. She's always like this before a big operation."

"It's a good thing I didn't ask her about my shoes. . . ."

Keller looked around to make sure there was nothing they were forgetting. Then she looked at the other three girls. They smiled back at her, eyes alert and ready for anything. Even the smallest one, who looked like a Christmas tree angel somebody had taken down and brought to life.

"Okay, people," Keller said. "This is it. It's showtime."

CHAPTER 15

Galen was wearing a dark sweater and pants that set off his blondness. It was casual but still appropriate for the promise ceremony later on. His eyes met Keller's briefly as Iliana said goodbye to her parents, and they both smiled. Not fake smiles, either. Simply the quiet, undemanding smiles of comrades with a job to do.

"Kee-kee!" Alex said from the door as they went to the car in the garage.

That kid is up *way* too late, Keller thought. She turned and waved.

"Blow him a kiss," Iliana prompted helpfully. "He likes that."

Keller gave her a narrow sideways look and blew him a kiss.

"Kee-kee!" Suddenly, his round little face crumpled. "Bye-bye," he proclaimed sadly.

"Oh, that's sweet," Iliana's mother said. "He's going to miss you. He probably thinks you're going for good."

"Bye-bye," Alex said, and huge tears rolled down his cheeks. "Bye-bye! Kee-kee! Bye-bye!" He began to sob.

There was a little silence among the group standing by the car. Winnie stared at Alex, then glanced at Iliana.

"He doesn't—he's never had any precognitions, has he?" she muttered.

"He's a *baby*," Iliana whispered back. "I mean, how could you tell?"

"He's just tired," Keller said briefly. "Come on, let's go."

But she could hear Alex's sobbing even when she got in the car, and it seemed to follow in her head even when they had left the house behind.

They checked with the "road crew" stationed right outside the Ashton-Hugheses' front gate. It looked extremely professional, with bright lights and all the accoutrements.

"All secure," the witch in charge said cheerfully when Keller rolled down the window. He shifted his reflective vest. "Thirty cars in, nobody out. There hasn't been one for a while—I think you're fashionably late." He winked.

"Thirty?" Keller said. "How many people per car?"

"Two in most of them, but some were packed."

Keller glanced at Iliana beside her. "And that's what they call only inviting a few people?"

Iliana shrugged. "You haven't seen the house."

"Anyway, it's safe," the witch foreman said. "No dragon has gotten in, I can promise you that. And none is going to *get* in, either."

Keller nodded at him, and they drove on.

Iliana was right. In considering how big the party was, you had to see the size of the house. Keller had studied the plans, but it wasn't the same.

They passed something like a peach orchard on one side of the driveway, and then a carriage house that seemed to have swallowed up a dozen cars. But Nissa dropped them off by the front steps, below the stately white columns that decorated the magnificent porch.

Impressive place, Keller thought.

They walked in.

In the cavernous, softly lit entry hall, there was a girl in a dark uniform who took their coats. There was also Brett. When he saw Iliana, he pounced.

"Blondie! I thought you weren't going to make it!"

"You knew I wouldn't miss this," Iliana said gently. But Keller thought she looked much less interested in Brett than the last time she'd spoken to him.

She's learned a lot, Keller thought. And, of course, now that she knows Galen, she sees this loser for what he is.

Brett was looking the others over in his meat-appraising way. "So just which of these lovely ladies is your cousin? I never got a chance to ask."

"Oh . . . that one." Iliana pointed a random finger.

"You?" Brett's eves ran up and down Keller's tallness and her blue-black hair. "I never would have guessed."

"We're sort of . . . foster cousins," Keller said.

She didn't like Brett. That was nothing new, but somehow tonight she *really* didn't like him. There was something almost creepy in the way his eyes clung to girls, and when he looked at Iliana, it was like watching a slug crawl over a peach blossom.

"Well, come with me and join the fun," he said, gesturing expansively and flashing a smile.

Keller almost asked "Where?" but in a moment she realized that it was pointless. The party really seemed to be all over the house.

The entry room itself was big enough to have a party in, and it had a wide, sweeping staircase just like a proper Southern mansion. Above, on the second floor, Keller could see a hallway lined with portraits and statues.

Brett led them through room after room, each one impressive. Some seemed to be real sitting rooms; others just looked like displays in a museum. Finally, they went through one last open archway into a ballroom.

Paneled walls. Painted ceiling. Chandeliers. An ocean of floor. And the college band at one end playing music that was definitely modern. A few couples were dancing a slow dance, very near the band. They looked small enough to rattle in the enormous room. Keller almost giggled, but Iliana looked dreamy.

"It's beautiful."

Brett looked satisfied. "There's food over there on the sideboard. But most of the food's downstairs in the game room. You want to see that?"

"I want to see Jaime," Iliana said.

"She's down there."

The game room was amazing, too. Not just pool tables and darts but arcade-style video games, old-fashioned pinball machines, an indoor basketball hoop, and generally just about everything you'd find at a superior arcade.

As soon as they walked in, a guy in black pants, white shirt, and black vest offered them a tray of tiny quiches and mini-pizzas. A caterer, Keller decided, not part of the regular staff of the house. She shook her head at the food and went on looking around, keeping her senses open so she could take in everything at once.

This was the first time Iliana had been out in public since she'd gone to school last Monday, and it was nerve-wracking. The game room was much more crowded than the ballroom, and everybody was laughing and talking at once. On top of that, this old mansion had some very modern renovations. The band music was being piped into the other rooms.

"Jaime!" Iliana said as a figure emerged from the crush of people.

Jaime looked good. Her face had a healthy color, and her dark blue eyes were wide open and shining. Her brown hair was fluffed softly, and she was wearing a very pretty blue dress.

"Iliana." She hugged Iliana hard, speaking in her flat but oddly pleasant voice. "It seems like forever. How are you?"

"Fine. My cold's better, and my hand—" Iliana held up her right hand. There was a neat bandage around the palm to protect the stitches. "It itches sometimes, but that's all. How about you?"

"I still have headaches. But I'm getting better." Jaime smiled at Keller and the others. "I'm so glad you all could come."

"Yeah, so are we," Keller said politely, feeling a stab of instinctive guilt. It was irrational, but she kept expecting this girl to look at her and say, "You're the one who attacked me! The monster cat!"

And she wasn't glad that they had come. Her early warning system was clamoring already; she felt as if her fur was standing on end. She couldn't explain it, but there was something *wrong* about the house.

"Keep alert," she said quietly to the others as Jaime led Iliana to the food tables. "Remember, two of us are with her at all times. The other two can wander the house, check the perimeter, look for anything suspicious. And keep in touch." She put a finger to her brooch.

That was when they found that their transmitters didn't work. Keller had no idea why. All any of them could hear was static like white noise.

Keller cursed.

"We'll keep in touch *physically*, then," she said grimly. She checked her watch. It was almost nine. "And we'll get her out of here in an hour. Ten o'clock. Just to be safe."

"Good idea," Galen said.

Winnie and Nissa said, "Right, Boss."

Keller stuck close to Iliana, telling herself that they were taking every precaution and that all she had to do was stay cool and they could get out safely. But as time went on, she only got more and more uneasy.

The dragon was going to attack.

She was certain of it.

But how? What form would the attack take? Was it going to be a battering ram of dark power like the one that had brought down the roof of the safe house? Or something tiny and sneaky, some clever way to get past the wards?

A mouse? Or an insect? No ordinary shapeshifter could turn into a bug, but it was a kind of animal, after all. Could something like that slip through the wards undetected?

What was it she was missing?

Nothing to do but keep her senses open, search every face for enemies, and be prepared for anything.

As it turned out, though, she was entirely unprepared when it happened.

Nissa and Galen were the two wandering the house at that point. Keller and Winnie were sticking with Iliana. Keller herself didn't plan to leave Iliana's side all night.

But as she was watching Jaime and Iliana laughing and chattering by one of the food tables—which offered everything from barbecue to shrimp to exotic fruit—Brett walked up chewing his lip. He was heading for Iliana, but he looked undecided and genuinely unhappy.

Keller headed him off reflexively. She preferred to keep him away from Iliana just on principle. "Anything wrong?"

He glanced at her with something like relief in his dark blue eyes. For once, he didn't look arrogant or patronizing or even well groomed. "Uh, there's something . . . I need to tell Iliana about . . . I guess." He gulped, his face twisted.

"You guess?" Keller herded him into a relatively private niche beside a video game. "What do you mean, you guess?"

"Well, I do have to tell her. I just hate to." He lowered his voice so that Keller had to lean closer to hear him. "Her mom's on the phone. And she says that her little brother is missing."

Ice water sluiced over Keller. For five seconds, she didn't breathe at all. Then she said, *"What?"*

Brett grimaced. "He's missing from his bedroom. And, I mean, I hate to scare Iliana with it, because he's probably just crawled out the window or something—he's that age, you know? But her mom wants to talk to her. She's sort of hysterical." He wet his lips. "I guess we should all go over there as a search party."

He's really worried, Keller thought dazedly, while another

part of her mind, a clear, cold part, clicked through possible solutions. So there's something under that brand-name facade after all. In spite of the "he probably crawled out of the window" crap, he's worried about the kid—and he's worried about telling Iliana, too.

Because Iliana's going to go ballistic, the cold part of her mind put in. She's going to get as hysterical as her mom and insist on rushing back there. And a search party—that would mean all of us outside the wards, crawling around between houses in the dark . . .

No. It couldn't happen. It was undoubtedly just what the dragon wanted.

But *how* had he gotten to the baby? With all those wards and the agents watching the house—how?

It didn't matter. Right now, she had to deal with the situation.

"Brett—don't tell Iliana."

"Huh? But I have to."

"No, you don't. I'll talk to Mrs.—to Aunt Anna. I'm her niece, remember? And I have an idea where the baby might have gone. I think he's safe, but she has to know where to look."

Brett gawked at her. "You have an idea?"

"Yeah. Just let me talk to her. And don't say anything to Iliana just yet." Keller glanced toward the game room bar, which was set up like an English pub. There was a phone, but a girl with red hair was talking animatedly into it, while eating nuts from a bowl.

"It's the other line, Jaime's line," Brett said. "She said she called on that one first, but it was busy."

"Okay, where's the other line?"

"Jaime's room."

Keller hesitated, looking at Iliana. Winnie was on one side of her and Jaime on the other. They were the center of attention, something like the heart of a rose, with other people surrounding them like petals.

At least she was in full view of everyone. And somebody trying to get to her would have to go through all of them first, and that would alert Winnie.

But I wish Nissa and Galen were here to take over from me.

She glanced at her watch. Fifteen minutes before they were supposed to come back to the game room. The baby couldn't wait that long.

She forged through the crowd and touched Winnie's shoulder.

"I have to run for a minute—a phone call. Nothing to worry about yet. I'll make it fast," she murmured in Winnie's ear.

Winnie glanced at her, surprised, but then she nodded. "Problems?"

"Maybe. Stay alert." Keller said it through a smile for Iliana's benefit.

When she got out of the throng, she said to Brett, "Take me there."

Actually, she knew where Jaime's bedroom was from the

plans. But she didn't want Brett hanging around Iliana. His face alone would give away the show.

They hurried up the wide staircase. Keller's mind was racing, making plans.

I can calm her down, at least. And I can call Circle Daybreak and tell them—if they don't already know. They'll make a much better search party than humans. Iliana doesn't need to know about it at all until after the ceremony. And then . . .

Her mind stalled, and the sick feeling in her stomach grew.

No. It wouldn't be enough. She knew what she really had to do.

I have to go back there. Just me. I owe Iliana that much. I owe the whole family that much.

I'll be the best one to search. I can drive over to the house fast and see what's going on. Borrow a car from Brett. That way, when the dragon attacks—and he's *going* to attack—I'll be the only one there.

You'll be the only one dead, a snide little voice in her mind pointed out. But Keller gave it the cold shoulder.

She knew that already. It wasn't important.

You're going to risk your life—give up your life—for a baby? One who's not a Wild Power, not even a shapeshifter?

At least I'll get another chance at the dragon, she told the voice.

You're going to risk the mission, the alliance, the whole

daylight world, for a single individual? the voice went on.

This was a better point. But Keller had only one thing to say to it.

I have to.

"Here." Brett gestured at the open door of a pretty bedroom, then followed Keller when she went in. "Um, can I help you?" He was getting over his worry and trying to cozy up to her again.

"No."

"Oh. Well, I'll leave you alone, then." He slid out the door, closing it behind him.

And Keller let him. Later, that was what she couldn't quite believe. That she had been stupid enough to walk into the trap and stand there while it snapped shut.

She picked up the phone. "Mrs. Dominick?"

Silence.

At first, just for a moment or two, she thought Iliana's mother might have stepped away from the phone. But then the nature of the silence got to her.

There were no sounds in the background at all. It was dead air.

Keller hit the plunger to hang up the phone. Nothing happened.

No dial tone.

She glanced at the phone cord; it was plugged into the wall. She pushed the plunger rapidly, four times, five.

Then she knew.

She'd been suckered.

In one motion, she whirled and sprang to the door.

Only to twist the handle uselessly.

It was locked.

And it was a good, sturdy door, made out of solid wood, the kind they used to make. She found this out by throwing herself against it hard enough to bruise her shoulder. It had been locked with a key from the outside, and the bolt was a good, sturdy one, too.

White icy-hot rage swept over Keller. She was more angry than she could ever remember being in her life. She couldn't believe it—she'd been fooled by an idiot human boy. The Night People must have gotten to him somehow, must have bought him . . .

No.

Keller knew she wasn't a genius. But sometimes ideas came to her in a flash, allowing her to see a complete picture all at once where other people saw only fragments. And right now, like a bolt of lightning, realization dawned on her, and she understood.

Oh, Goddess, how could we have been so stupid?

She knew how the dragon had done it.

CHAPTER 16

We were so careful, she thought, setting up wards three days early and having agents watch the house. Nothing got inside during those three days; we were sure of that, and so we thought we were safe.

But we didn't stop to think—what if the dragon was *already* inside when we put the wards up?

Brett.

He's the dragon.

It could take on any shape, assume any animal's form, and know all that the animal knew. A human being was an animal.

So why couldn't it touch a human and know all the human knew?

It would be the perfect disguise.

And we all fell for it, Keller thought. I knew there was

something creepy about him, but I just put it down to him being obnoxious. And he's been here all the time, inside the wards, laughing at us, waiting for Iliana to come.

And Iliana's with him right now.

Keller felt sure of that in her gut.

She wanted to throw herself against the door again, but that wouldn't do any good. She needed to be calm now, to think, because she couldn't afford to waste any time.

The window.

Keller tried to open it, looking down at a hedge of rhododendron bushes below. The sash was stuck, nailed fast. But it didn't matter. Glass was more breakable than wood.

She stepped back and changed.

Melting, flowing, jumpsuit becoming fur. Tail shooting free. Ears. Whiskers. Heavy paws thumping down. A single long stretch to get used to the new body and being on four feet instead of two.

She was a panther, and she felt good. Strong and mean. Her muscles were like steel under her soft coat, and her big paws were twitching to bat someone silly. That dragon would be sorry he'd ever messed with her.

With a rasping yowl that she couldn't help, she gathered herself and sprang straight at the window. The full weight of her panther body hit the glass, and it shattered, and then she was flying in the cold night air.

She got cut. Panthers actually had thin and delicate skin compared to other animals. But she was indifferent to the pain. She landed and took off running, shaking her paws in flight to get rid of little bits of glass.

She raced around the mansion, looking for a place to enter. Eventually, she found a low, unshuttered window, and once again, she gathered herself and jumped.

She landed in a sitting room with glass falling all around her onto a fine, old carpet.

Brett.

And Iliana.

She would smell them out.

She lifted her muzzle, smelling currents in the air. At the same time, she expanded her sense of hearing to its fullest.

No Iliana. She couldn't get even a whiff of her. That was bad, but she would try again from the game room, where Iliana had been last. That was where she was going anyway, because that was where Brett was.

Not Brett, she reminded herself as she loped through corridors and rooms. The dragon.

She raced through the ballroom and heard a scream. She barely turned her head to notice a girl standing frozen, just lifting her hand to point. The college band crashed to a halt, almost as one, except the drummer, who went on playing for a moment with his eyes shut.

Keller ignored them all, running at top speed and leaping down the stairs, her heavy front paws hitting the carpeted floor first, then her back paws hitting almost on either side of them. Each spring propelled her into the next.

She burst into the game room.

For an instant, she stood still, taking in the scene. She wanted to make sure with her eyes that what her ears and her nose told her was true: Iliana wasn't here.

It was true. Winnie was missing, too, and Keller couldn't smell them anywhere.

Then someone spotted her, a full-grown panther, jet-black, with glowing eyes and long teeth just showing as she panted gently, standing in the doorway with her tail lashing.

"Oh, my God!" The voice soared over the babble. "Look at that!"

Everyone looked.

Everyone froze for an instant.

Chaos erupted.

Girls were screaming. Boys were yelling. Plenty of boys were screaming, too. They saw her, and they fell over themselves, diving for the exits or for hiding places. They poured out of the room, dragging each other, sometimes trampling each other. Keller gave a loud, snarling yowl to help them on, and they scattered like chickens.

The only one Keller cared about was the Brett-dragon.

He turned and ran down a corridor. Luring her? He must

be. Maybe he didn't realize she had found out yet. Maybe he had some reason for continuing the charade.

She threw her head back and gave a snarl that resounded through the house. It wasn't just anger. It was calling Nissa and Galen. If they could hear her, they would understand and come running.

Then she took off after the dragon.

As she loped down the corridor, she changed again. This time, she couldn't just try to kill him; she needed to be able to talk. But she also needed her claws, so she changed to her half-and-half form, fur shriveling off her arms, body rearing up to run on booted feet, hair flying out behind her.

The dragon was almost at the end of the corridor when she jumped him.

She knocked him down and rolled him over, straddling him. She was braced to feel the agony of the dark power crackling through her, but it didn't come. She pinned his arms and showed her teeth and screamed in his face.

"Where is she? What did you do with her?"

The face looked back at her. It looked just like Brett, just like a human. It was sickly white, with rolling eyeballs and spittle at the corners of the mouth. The only answer she got was a moan of what sounded like terror.

"Tell me! Where is she?"

"—it's not my fault . . ."

"What?" She lifted his body and banged it down again.

His head flopped on his neck like a dead fish. He looked like someone about to faint.

Something was wrong.

"She's in the bedroom with my parents. They're all asleep—or something—"

His forehead. When she shook him, his hair flew around. It was uncharacteristically messy, but the forehead underneath was smooth.

"I couldn't help it. *He* did something to my brain. I couldn't even think until a few minutes ago. I just did what he told me to do. I was like a robot! And you don't know what it was like, having *him* in the house the last three days, and feeling like a puppet, and when *he* let go a few minutes ago, I thought I was going to be killed—"

The babbling went on, but Keller's mind had disengaged.

She had lots of thoughts all at once, like layers in a parfait.

Chalk up another ability for dragons: telepathic mind control. Of weak human subjects, anyway.

Nissa was right: the Night World did know what had happened in the music room. The substitution was probably made right after that. They could have grabbed Jaime on her way back to class.

The car incident was designed to make us sympathetic and to lull our suspicions before they began. We thought of her as a victim.

The doctors at the hospital must have been controlled,

too. They *had* to have been—they'd looked at Jaime's head.

Jaime's headaches have kept her at home for the past three days, so she never had to cross the wards.

Iliana trusts Jaime implicitly and would go anywhere with her without a fight.

Jaime wears bangs.

And on the last layer, rushing at her cold and sharp as crystal: Jaimeisthedragon.

Jaime is the dragon.

A vast, silent calm seemed to have filled Keller. She felt as if there was too much space inside her head. Very slowly, she looked down at Brett again.

"Stop talking." It was almost a whisper, but his gabble stopped as if she'd turned off a faucet.

"Now. Who's in the bedroom with your parents? Your sister?"

He nodded, terrified. Tears spurted out of his eyes.

"Your real sister."

He nodded again.

They must have brought her in sometime, Keller thought. Certainly before we put the wards up and started checking cars, maybe even before the fake Jaime got back from the hospital.

Why they'd kept her alive was a mystery, but Keller didn't have time to worry about it.

"Brett," she said, still in a careful whisper, "what I want to know is where *Iliana* is. Do you know where she's been taken?"

He choked. "I don't know. *He* didn't tell me anything, even when *he* was in my mind. But I noticed—there were some people down in the cellar. I think they were making a tunnel."

A tunnel. Under the wards, of course. So we were made fools of *twice.*

She had to grit her teeth to keep from screaming. The floor plan of the house was a blur in her mind.

She hauled Brett up by his shirt and said, "Where's the basement door? Show me!"

"I c-can't—"

"Move!"

He moved, staggering. She followed, pushing him along, until they got to a door and stairs.

Then he collapsed. "Down there. Don't ask me to go with you. I can't. I can't look at *him* again." He huddled, rocking himself.

Keller left him. Three stairs down, she bounded back up and grabbed him by the shirt.

"That phone call from Iliana's mother—does *he* really have the baby?" She needed to know if it came to bargaining.

"I don't know," Brett moaned in a sick voice. He was clutching his stomach as if he were wounded. "There wasn't any phone call, but I don't know what *he's* been doing." He threw her a desperate look and whispered hoarsely, *"What is he?"*

Keller dropped him. "You don't want to know," she said, and left him again.

She took the stairs very quietly but very quickly. Her senses were open, but the farther she went down, the less useful they were. They were being swamped by an overpowering sickly-sweet odor and by a rushing sound that seemed to fill her head.

By the time she got to the last step, her fur was bristling, and her heart was pounding. Her tail stood out stiffly, and her pupils were wide.

It was very dark, but details of the room slowly came into focus. It was a large furnished basement, or had been. Now every piece of furniture seemed to be broken and piled in a heap in the corner. There was a raw hole in one concrete wall, a hole that opened into a black tunnel. And the sickly-sweet smell came from piles of dung.

They were lying on the floor all around, along with giant scratch marks that had dug grooves into the tile. The entire place looked like nothing so much as a huge animal's den.

She couldn't sense anything alive in the room.

Keller moved toward the tunnel, fast but stealthy. Ripple, freeze. Ripple, freeze. Leopards could move this way across grassland bare of cover and not be seen. But nothing jumped out to attack her.

The mouth of the tunnel was wet, the soil crumbly. Keller climbed in, still moving lightly. Water dripped from the mat of roots and earth above her. The whole thing looked ready to cave in at any moment.

He must have made it. The dragon. Goddess knows how; maybe with claws. Anyway, he wasn't too fussy about it; it was meant to be a temporary thing.

The smell was just as powerful here, and the rushing sound was even clearer. There must be an underground stream—or maybe just water pipes—very close.

Come on, girl, what are you waiting for? You're a grunt, it's your job to move! Don't stand around trying to think!

It was hard to make herself go deeper and deeper into that damp and confining place. Her senses were all useless, even sight, because the bore twisted and turned so she could never see more than a few feet ahead. She was heading blind and deaf into she had no idea what. At any moment, she might reach a shaft or a side tunnel where something could attack her.

And the feel of the earth above her was almost crushing.

She kept going.

Please let her be alive. He doesn't need to kill her. He should try to make her join him first. Please, please, don't let him have killed her.

After what seemed like forever, she realized that the angle of the tunnel was changing. She was heading up. Then a current of air swirled to her, barely sniffable under the thick dragon smell, and it was fresh.

Night air. Somewhere ahead. The end of the tunnel.

A new panic invaded her.

Please don't let them have gotten away.

She threw aside all caution and sprinted.

Up, up—and she could smell it clearly now. Cold air, unfouled. Up, up—and she could hear sounds. A yell that suddenly broke off. The voice sounded like—

Galen! she thought, and her heart tore.

Then she saw light. Moonlight. She gathered her muscles and *jumped.*

She scrambled out of the mouth of the tunnel.

And there, in moonlight that hurt her eyes, she saw everything.

A car, a black Jeep, parked under a tree. The engine running but the seats empty. And in front of it, what looked like a battlefield.

There were bodies everywhere. Several were vampires in black—dark ninjas. But also on the ground were the bodies of Nissa and Winnie and Galen.

So they followed, a distant part of Keller's mind said, not interfering in the slightest with the part that was getting ready for the fight. They followed the dragon—which must have done something to Winnie to get Iliana away from her. That was why I couldn't smell anybody; they all went into the tunnel while I was upstairs with brother Brett.

She couldn't tell if they were dead. They were all lying very still, and there was blood on Winnie's head and on Nissa's right arm and back. Blood and claw marks.

And Galen . . . he was sprawled out full-length, with no

signs of breathing. He wasn't even a warrior. He'd never had a chance.

Then Keller saw something that drove the others out of her head.

The dragon.

It was standing near the Jeep, but frozen, as if it had just wheeled to face her. It was holding a limp figure in silvery-white casually, almost tucked under its arm.

And it still looked like Jaime Ashton-Hughes.

It was wearing Jaime's pretty blue dress. Its soft brown hair blew gently about its face, and Keller could feel its dark blue eyes fixed on her.

But there were differences, too. Its skin was deadly pale, and something yellowish was oozing from a cut on its cheekbone. Its lips were drawn back from its teeth in a grinning snarl that Jaime never could have managed. And when the wind blew the soft hair off its forehead, Keller could see horns.

There they were. Stubby and soft-looking—or at least soft on the outside, like downy skin over bone. They were so obviously real and yet so grotesque that Keller felt her stomach turn.

And there were five of them.

Five.

The book said one to three! Keller thought indignantly. And in rare cases four. But this *thing* has five! Five seats of shapeshifting power, not to mention the black energy, mind control, and whatever else it's been keeping up its sleeve just for me.

I'm dead.

Well, she had known that from the beginning, of course. She'd known it six days ago when she first leaped for the dragon's back in the mall. But now the realization was more bitter, because not only was she dead, so was all hope.

I can't kill that thing. It's going to slaughter me as easily as the others. And then take Iliana.

It didn't matter. She had to try.

"Put the girl down," she said. She kept her half-and-half shape to say it. Maybe she could startle it by changing suddenly when she sprang.

"I don't think so," the dragon said with Jaime's mouth. It had Jaime's voice down perfectly. But then it opened the mouth, and basso profundo laughter came out, so deep and startling that Keller felt ice down her spine.

"Come on," Keller said. "Neither of us wants her hurt." While she was talking, she was moving slowly, trying to circle behind it. But it turned with her, keeping its back to the Jeep.

"You may not," the dragon said. "But I really don't care. She's already hurt; I don't know if she'll make it anyway." Its grin spread wider.

"Put her down," Keller said again. She knew that it wouldn't. But she wanted to keep talking, keep it off guard.

She also knew it wasn't going to let her get behind it.

Panthers naturally attack from behind. It wasn't going to be an option.

Keller's eyes shifted to the huge and ancient pine tree the Jeep was parked under. Or they didn't actually shift, because that would have given the dragon a clue. She expanded her awareness to take it in.

It was her chance.

"We haven't even properly introduced ourselves—" she began.

And then, in midsentence, she leaped.

CHAPTER 17

Not for the dragon. She jumped for the tree.

It was a good, tall loblolly pine, whose drooping lower branches didn't look as if they could support a kitten. But Keller didn't need support. As she leaped, she changed, pushing it as fast as she could. She reached the tree with four paws full of lethal claws extended.

And she ran straight up the vertical surface. Her claws sank into the clean, cinnamon trunk, and she shot up like a rocket. When she got high enough to be obscured by the dull-green needles on the droopy branches, she launched herself into the air again.

It was a desperate move, betting everything on one blind spring. But it was all she could think of. She could never take the dragon in a fair fight.

She was betting on her claws.

In the wild, a panther could shear the head off a deer with a single swipe.

Keller was going for the horns.

She came down right on target. The dragon made the mistake of looking up at her, maybe thinking that she was trying to get behind it, to land on its back again and kill it. Or maybe thinking that she might see the pale face of an innocent girl and hesitate.

Whatever it thought, it was a mistake.

Keller was already slashing as she landed. A single deadly swipe with all her power behind it. Her claws peeled the forehead off the creature in a spray of blood and flesh.

The screaming roar almost burst her eardrums.

It was the sound she'd heard before in the mall, a sound so deep in pitch that she felt it as much as heard it. It shook her bones, and it reverberated in every tree and in the red clay of the ground.

And that was another mistake, although Keller didn't know it at once.

At the same instant as she heard the roar, she felt the pain. The dark power crackled through her like a whiplash and tore her own involuntary scream from her. It was worse than the first time she'd felt it, ten times worse, maybe more. The dragon was much stronger.

And it followed her.

Like a real whip, it flashed across the clearing after her. It hit her again as she hit the ground, and Keller screamed again.

It *hurt.*

She tried to scrabble away, but the pain made her weak, and she fell over on her side. And then the black energy hit her right shoulder—exactly where it had hit the first time in the mall.

Keller saw white light.

And then she was falling in darkness.

Her last thought was, I didn't get it. I couldn't have. It still has power.

Iliana, I'm sorry . . .

She stopped feeling anything.

She opened her eyes slowly.

Hurts . . .

She was looking up at the dragon.

It had dropped Iliana; Keller couldn't see where. And it was staring down at her in malevolent fury, obviously waiting for her to wake up so she could feel it when it killed her.

When *he* killed her. He'd taken on the shape he'd been wearing in the beginning. A young man with clean, handsome features and a nicely muscled if compact body. Black hair that shed rainbow colors under the moonlight and looked as fine and soft as her own fur. And those obsidian eyes.

It was hard to look away from those eyes. They seemed to capture her gaze and suck her in. They were so much more like stones than eyes, silver-black, shiny stones that seemed to reflect all light out again.

But when she managed to drag her gaze upward, she felt a thrill of hope. His forehead was a bleeding ruin.

She *had* gotten him. Her slash had carved a nice hamburger-sized piece out of his scalp. Somewhere on the ground in the clearing were two little stubby horns.

But only two; there were three left on his head. He must have turned at the last instant. Keller would have cursed if she had a human throat.

"How're you feeling?" the dragon said, and leered at her form under the gory mess of his scalp.

Keller tried to snarl at him and realized that she *did* have a human throat. She must have collapsed back into her half-and-half form, and she was too weak to change back again.

"Having trouble?" the dragon asked.

Keller croaked, "You should never have come back."

"Wrong," the dragon said. "I like the modern world."

"You should have stayed asleep. Who woke you up?" She was buying time, of course, to try and regain some strength. But she also truly wanted to know.

The dragon laughed. "Someone," he said. "Someone you'll never know. A witch who isn't a witch. We made our own alliance."

Keller didn't understand, and her brain was too fuzzy to deal with it. But just at that moment, she noticed something else.

Movement behind the dragon. The figures that had been

lying on the ground were stirring. And they were doing it stealthily, in ways that showed they were awake and with their wits about them.

They were *alive.* She could see Galen's head lift, with moonlight shining on his hair as he looked at her. She could see Winnie turn toward Iliana and begin to crawl. She could see Nissa's shoulders hump and then fall back.

Later, when they were asked, they would all say the same thing had brought them to awareness: a deep rumbling sound that vibrated in their bones. The dragon's roar.

Or, at least, three of them would say that. Galen would always say that all he heard was Keller's scream and his eyes came open.

The surge of hope she felt made Keller's heart beat hard and wiped away the pain—for the moment, at least. But she was terrified of giving the dragon some clue.

She didn't dare look at Galen any longer. She stared at the dragon's black stone eyes and thought with all her strength, Get away.

Get away, take the Jeep, take Iliana. He may not be able to follow you. *Run.*

"Your time's over," she told the dragon out loud. "The shapeshifters don't want you anymore. Everything has changed."

"And it's changing again," the dragon said. "The end of the world is coming, and the beginning of a new one. It's time for everything that's sleeping to wake back up again."

Keller had a horrified vision of hundreds of dragons being dug up and brought back to life. But there was something going on in the clearing that was even more horrifying to her.

Galen wasn't getting away. He was slithering on his stomach toward her.

And Winnie, the idiot, was beside Iliana now—but she wasn't dragging her to the Jeep. She seemed to be whispering to her.

Keller felt a hot wave of utter desperation.

What can I do?

If the dragon sees them, they're all dead. There's nothing any of them can do against him. Galen's not a warrior—he can't change. Nissa looks too hurt to move. Winnie's orange fire won't even singe the dragon. And Iliana will get swatted like a butterfly.

They can't do anything. I have to.

She was so tired and hurt, and her claws were much less lethal than in her full panther form. But she had to do it, and she had to do it *now.*

"Go back where you came from!" she shouted. She bunched her muscles and jumped.

Right for him. Straight on. That was what took him by surprise, the sheer insanity of the attack. He threw the black energy at her, but he couldn't stop her leap.

Her claws ripped into his forehead again, and then she fell back.

The dragon's scream split the heavens. Dizzy with pain and shock, Keller stared at him, hoping desperately . . .

But she'd taken only one horn off. He still had two.

He thrashed around in wounded fury, then threw the dark power at her again. Keller shuddered and lost her balance. She crashed to the ground and lay there, limp.

"Keller!" The scream was full of such raw anguish that it hurt Keller's throat to hear it. It made her heart throb hard and then fall in sick dismay.

Galen, no, she thought. Don't bother with me. You have to get Iliana away.

"Keller!" he screamed again, and then he was beside her, holding her.

"No . . . ," she whispered.

She couldn't say more than that. She looked at him pleadingly with the eyes of a dumb beast. If he died, too, it would make her own death meaningless.

The dragon was still screaming, both hands to his forehead. He seemed to be too angry to attack.

"Keller, hang on. Please, you have to hang on." Galen was dripping tears on her face.

"Run . . . ," she whispered.

Instead, he did the most gallant thing she had ever seen.

He was already holding her, his shaky hand stroking the hair off her face, brushing one of her tufted ears. Now, suddenly, he gripped her hard, and his expression changed.

His jaw tightened, and a white line showed around his mouth. And his eyes . . . seemed to darken and glow red.

Too late, Keller realized.

He was taking her impression. Learning her shape.

No. You were meant to be something gentle.

Galen stood up.

And changed.

But something was a little off. Maybe it was the fact that he had to hurry when he took the impression, or some extra twist from his own genes. Because, instead of becoming a soot-black panther, he became a gleaming golden leopard.

The same animal. Different colors. This leopard was the dark rich gold of Galen's hair, and its eyes were the incredible green of his eyes.

He was marked with perfect black rosettes, each with an even darker gold center. His body was sleek and supple and almost seven feet long with the tail. He was a *big* leopard, at least a hundred and sixty pounds.

And before Keller had time to think, he was in motion.

A good spring. Untutored but full of the real killer instinct. The coughing yell he let out as he jumped was the kind a cat makes when its fury is too great to hold in.

The dragon whirled to face him. But it was too late. Once again, the crackling dark power hit but couldn't stop the rush. The dragon's human body couldn't fend off a hundred and sixty pounds of solid feline muscle.

Keller saw Galen swipe.

The dragon bellowed, clapping a hand to his head.

And Keller wanted to cheer.

She couldn't. She didn't have the strength left. But her heart was singing inside her with sheer pride.

You did it. Oh, Galen, my *prince*, you did it.

She saw his body falling, struck by the black energy. She saw it hit the ground and lie still.

And she was sorry that they were both going to die. But with the dragon dead, too, and Iliana alive, there would still be hope. There would be people to carry on.

Then she looked at the dragon, and time stopped, and her heart turned to ice.

He still had a horn left. The one right in the middle.

They hadn't done it after all.

He still had power. He was going to kill them now, and Iliana, too. And neither she nor Galen could do anything to stop him.

The noises the dragon was making were beyond description. He seemed to be out of his mind in pain and fury. And then Keller realized that it was more than that. He was screaming in sheer blood-lust—and he was changing.

So strange—she hadn't even thought about the dragon changing before. But she could take on most animals. She knew to go for the juncture between head and neck for rhinos, the belly for a lion.

But this . . . what it was shifting into . . .

No.

I don't believe it, Keller thought.

It looked more like a moth being born than a shapeshifter changing. It split its human skin like a chrysalis. More of the yellowish liquid she had seen on Jaime's cheek oozed from the splits. And what was revealed underneath was hard and greenish-yellow, flat, smooth.

Scaly.

The smell was the smell from the basement. Sickly-sweet, pungent, an odor to make your stomach lurch.

Powerful back legs bunched, and the figure grew and stood against the moonlit sky.

It was huge.

In her mind, Keller saw a scene from the past. Iliana, her violet eyes huge, saying, "He can turn into a *dragon*?"

And Keller's scornful answer, "No, of course not. Don't be silly."

Wrong, Keller thought.

It actually looked more like velociraptor than a dragon. Too big—it was more than fifteen feet long, counting the powerful tail. But it had the same look of alien intelligence, the same reptilian snout, the same saberlike hind claws.

It's not a mindless animal, Keller thought. It's smart. It even has things like hands on its forelegs. It's where evolution took a different turn.

And it had power. Maybe more power this way than in its human form. Keller could feel its mind even at this distance, the terrible ancient core of hatred and malice, the endless thirst for blood.

It opened its mouth, and for an instant Keller expected to see fire. But what came out was a roar that showed huge spiky teeth—and a flood of black energy. The dark power crackled around it like an aura of lightning.

Nothing—no shapeshifter, no witch, no vampire—could stand against this creature. Keller knew that absolutely.

That was when she saw Iliana getting up.

Stay down, you idiot! Keller thought.

Iliana stood straight.

There's no point, don't attract its attention . . .

"Azhdeha!" Iliana shouted.

And the monster turned.

There they were, the maiden and the dragon, face-to-face. Iliana looked twice as small as ever before in contrast to this giant. Her silver-gold hair was blowing loose in the wind, and her dress shimmered around her. She was so delicate, so graceful—and so fragile, standing there like a lily swaying on its stalk.

I can't watch, Keller thought. I can't see this. Please . . .

"Azhdeha!" Iliana said, and her voice was sweet but ringing and stern. "Hashteher! Tiamat!"

It's a spell, Keller thought. Winnie taught her a spell?

When they were lying there, whispering together? But what kind of spell would Winnie know against dragons?

"Poisonous Serpent! Cold-blooded Biter! Rastaban! Anguis!"

No, they're names, Keller realized slowly. *Its* names. Dragon names.

Old names.

"I am a witch and the daughter of a witch. Mine was the hand that took your power; mine was the hand that buried you in silence. Hecate was the most ancient of my mothers. Hecate's hand is my hand now."

Winnie couldn't have taught her that. *Nobody* could have taught her that. No witch alive today.

Keller could see Winnie's pale face watching in surprise from beyond Iliana, her eyes and mouth dark O's.

"Mine is the hand that *sends you back*!"

Iliana's palms were cupped now, and orange fire crackled between them.

Keller's heart plummeted.

Golden-orange fire. Witch fire. It was impressive, from a girl who'd never been trained, but it wasn't nearly enough. It was about as dangerous to the dragon as a firefly.

She heard Winnie's voice in the silence, small and frightened but determined.

"Aim for the horn!"

The dragon threw back its head and laughed.

That was what it looked like, anyway. What came out was a roar like all the other roars and a belch of black energy that fountained skyward. But in her head, Keller heard maniacal laughter.

Then it swung its head back down and pointed the horn straight at Iliana.

Die! it said. The word wasn't spoken but sent on a cold wave of pure energy.

"Mine is the power of the ages!" Iliana shouted back. *"Mine is the power—"*

The golden flare in her palms was changing, blazing white, blinding hot . . .

"—OF THE END OF THE WORLD!"

Something like a supernova was born between her hands.

The light shot up and out, exploding. It was impossible to look at. And it was no longer white but dazzling, lightning-brilliant blue.

The blue fire.

The Wild Power had awakened.

I knew it, Keller thought. I knew it all along.

Keller couldn't see what happened to the dragon; the light was simply too bright. While it flared around her, she was bathed in radiance that seemed to shine *through* her, humming inside her and lighting up her bones. She tried to lift her own hand and saw nothing but a vague rainbow shape.

But she heard the dragon's scream. Not low like the roar

but high and squealing, a sound like icicles driving into her ears. It went up and up, higher in pitch until even Keller couldn't track it. And then there was a thin sound like distant glass shattering, and then there was no sound at all.

There were shooting stars in the blue-white light.

For the second time that evening, Keller fainted.

"Boss! Please, Boss, hurry. Wake up!"

Keller blinked open her eyes. Galen was holding her. He was human. So was she.

And Winnie and Nissa were trying to drag both of them somewhere.

Keller gazed up into those gold-green eyes. The exact color of a leopard's, she thought. Only leopards don't cry, and his were brimming with tears.

She lifted a languorous hand and stroked his cheek. He cupped his own hand over it.

Keller couldn't think. There were no words in her mind. But she was glad to be here with him, for this last moment in the moonlight. It had all been worth it

"Boss, *please*!" Winnie was almost crying, too.

"Let me die in peace," Keller said, although she didn't realize she was saying it aloud until she heard the words. Then she added, "Don't *you* cry, Winfrith. You did a good job."

"Boss, you're not dying! The blue fire did something—it healed us. We're all okay. *But it's almost midnight!*"

Keller blinked. She blinked again.

Her body didn't hurt anymore. She'd assumed it was the blessed numbness that comes just before death. But now she realized that it wasn't. Her blood was running in her veins; her muscles felt firm and strong. She didn't even have a headache.

She stared beyond Winnie to the girl in white.

Iliana was still slight and childlike, almost fairylike of figure. But something had changed about her. At first, Keller thought she looked as distant and beautiful as a star, but then she smiled and wasn't distant at all. She was simply more beautiful than the dreams of mortals.

And *really* shining with her own light. It pooled around her in soft, silvery radiance. Keller had never seen a Wild Power do that before, not on any of the tapes.

But she's not just a Wild Power, the voice in her head whispered. She's the Witch Child.

And Goddess alone knows all that she's meant to do.

For a moment, Keller felt so awed that it was almost like unhappiness. But then Winnie's message finally sank in.

She snapped her head up. "Midnight?"

"Yes!" Winnie said frantically.

Keller bolted upright. "Nissa?"

"Right here, Boss."

Keller felt a flood of relief. Nissa was the one who had seemed closest to death on the ground there. But now she was standing on her own two feet, looking cool and imperturbable, even though her shirt was bloody and in rags.

"Nissa, can you drive that Jeep? Can you figure out how to get to Charlotte?"

"I think so, Boss."

Keller had never been so grateful to hear that calm voice in her life. She jumped up.

"Then let's go!"

CHAPTER 18

The ride to Charlotte passed in a blur. All Keller could remember was hanging on while Nissa did some of the wildest driving she'd ever experienced. They went off-road for a good deal of the way.

It was one minute to midnight when they squealed into a parking lot in front of a long, low building.

"Go in, go in!" Nissa said, slamming to a stop in front of a set of double doors.

Keller and Galen and Winnie and Iliana ran.

They burst into a large room that seemed very brightly lit. A sea of chairs with bodies sitting in them swam in front of Keller's eyes. Then she focused on a platform at the front.

"Come on," she said tersely.

There were a number of people sitting at a table on the platform, facing the audience just like any ordinary panel, with glasses of water and microphones in front of them. But Keller recognized some of the people as she got closer, and they were anything but ordinary.

That little dumpling-shaped woman with the round face was Mother Cybele. Mother of all the Witches, just as Grandma Harman had been Crone. With Grandma Harman dead, she was the witches' leader.

The tall girl with the lovely features and the café au lait skin who sat beside her was Aradia. The blind Maiden of the Witches mentioned in the prophecies.

And that regal-looking man with the golden hair and beard, sitting by the queenly woman with flashing green eyes . . .

They could only be the leaders of the First House of the shapeshifters.

Galen's mother and father.

There were others, too, important people from Circle Daybreak, but Keller didn't have time to focus on them. Mother Cybele was on her feet and speaking. She must have been a little short-sighted, because she didn't appear to see Keller and the others coming up on the side. Her voice was slow and concerned.

"I'm afraid that since it's now past midnight—"

Keller glanced at her watch. "It's just midnight now!"

Mother Cybele looked up, startled, over her glasses. Every head on the panel turned. And every face in the audience was suddenly fixed on Keller's group.

A low murmur like the humming of bees began, but it swelled very quickly to something like a muted roar. People were pointing openly as Keller ran up the steps to the stage.

She glanced back at the others and realized why. They were a pretty sad-looking bunch. Every one of them was dirty and ragged. Winnie's strawberry blond hair was dark red with blood on one side. Galen's sweater was in shreds. And she herself was filthy from the tunnel and all the dirt she'd encountered in the clearing.

Only Iliana looked reasonably clean, and that was probably because the glow kept you from focusing too closely.

Mother Cybele gave a little cry of joy that sounded quite young, and she dropped the index cards she'd been holding. Aradia stood up, her beautiful blank eyes turned toward them, her entire face shining with joy. Galen's parents looked extremely startled and relieved.

But some guy in a dark suit grabbed Keller's arm as she reached the top of the steps.

"Who are you supposed to be?" he said.

Keller shook him off and stood with her hair swirling around her. "We're the people who're bringing you the Wild Power," she said. She spotted Nissa just coming in the door and beckoned to her. "And we're also the ones who killed the dragon."

The big room fell so silent that you could have heard a paper clip drop.

"Well, actually, *she* killed the dragon," Keller said, pointing to Iliana.

Aradia said in a hushed voice, "The Witch Child. She's come to us."

Iliana walked slowly up onto the stage and stood straight. "I didn't kill it alone," she said. "Everybody helped, and especially Keller and Galen."

Galen's father's golden eyebrows went up, and Galen's mother gripped her husband's arm. Keller glanced sideways at Galen and saw that he was blushing.

"They fought it and fought it until they were both almost dead. But then, when I used the blue fire, they got better again."

She said it so simply, speaking to Mother Cybele alone, or so it seemed. She didn't look in the least self-conscious, or in the least arrogant.

I suppose she's used to having everybody looking at her, Keller thought.

Mother Cybele actually clasped her little soft hands together and shut her eyes. When she opened them again, they were shining with tears.

But all she said was, "Welcome, my child. Grandma Harman's last words were for you. She hoped you would find your power."

"She did," Keller said. "Winnie helped her."

"I didn't help her do *that*," Winnie said candidly. "What she did back there and what she said. I just tried to show her how to use the orange fire. But when she started talking—"

She shook her curly head. "I don't know where she got all that stuff about Hecate."

"It just came to me," Iliana said. "I don't know. It was as if somebody were saying it to me, and I was just repeating it."

But who could have said it? Keller thought. Who else but somebody who was there the first time, when the dragons were put to sleep? Who else but Hecate Witch-Queen herself?

Even though she'd been dead thirty thousand years.

It's time for everything that's sleeping to wake back up again.

Keller realized that she was hearing a noise from the crowd. At first, she thought that they were muttering in disbelief again, or maybe in annoyance at these people who were standing on the stage and chattering.

Then it got louder and louder, and she realized it was applause.

People were clapping and cheering and whistling. It was echoing off the ceiling and walls. And just when Keller thought it couldn't possibly get any louder, a new wave would come and prove her wrong.

It took a long time for Mother Cybele to get them all quieted down. Then she turned to Keller and said formally, "So you've completed your mission?"

Keller realized that it was a cue. And in the midst of the dizzy happiness she'd been feeling, something twisted in her heart.

She kept it from showing on her face. She kept herself standing erect.

"Yes," she said to Mother Cybele. "I've brought the Witch Child." She swallowed hard.

"And here is the son of the First House of the shapeshifters," Galen's father said. He stepped over to Galen and took his hand. His face was stern but glowing with pride.

Galen's face was pale but set. He looked at Keller—for just one moment. And then he looked straight out at the audience with unseeing eyes.

Mother Cybele looked toward Iliana. To take *her* hand, Keller supposed, and join it with Galen's. But Iliana was holding some whispered conversation with Aradia.

When she finally turned around, Iliana said, "I want Keller to do it. She's the one responsible for all this."

Keller blinked. Her throat was so swollen, it was impossible to swallow again. But she wouldn't have thought it of Iliana. Really, it seemed so pointlessly cruel to make *her* do it.

But maybe she doesn't understand. That's it, she doesn't realize, Keller thought. She let out a careful, shaky breath and said, "Okay."

She reached for Iliana's hand—

And felt a stab in her palm.

She looked down, astonished. Iliana had a *knife* in that hand, a perfectly serviceable little knife. She had cut Keller with it, and Keller was bleeding. In fact, Iliana seemed to be bleeding, too.

"Sorry," Iliana hissed. "Ick, I hate blood."

Then, grabbing Keller's hand again, she faced the audience and raised it up high.

"There!" she said. "Now we're blood sisters. And she's already been like a sister to me, because she saved my life over and over. And if *that's* not good enough for an alliance between the witches and the shapeshifters, I don't know what is."

The entire audience gaped at her. Mother Cybele blinked rapidly.

"Are you saying . . . ?" Galen's father looked incredulous. "Are you saying that you won't marry my son?"

"I'm saying that *she* ought to marry your son—or promise to him, or whatever they want. She's the one he's in love with. And I don't see why you should make him miserable for his whole life just because you want the shapeshifters tied to the witches. Keller and I are tied together, and we always will be. And Galen, too. Why can't that be enough?"

A sound was starting from the crowd again. Keller's heart seemed to soar on it. But she was still staring at Iliana, afraid to believe.

"But . . . what if the witches don't agree to it?" Galen's father said feebly.

Iliana stamped her foot. She actually did.

"I'm the *Witch Child.* They'd better listen to me. I didn't go through all of this for nothing."

Then the crowd was thundering applause even louder than before, and the wave seemed to sweep Keller right into Galen's arms.

Sometime later, in the middle of a lot of hugging and kissing, Keller whispered to Iliana, "Are you sure?"

"I'd better be sure, don't you think? Or Galen's going to be pretty upset."

"Iliana—"

"I'm sure," Iliana whispered. She squeezed Keller. "I really do care about him. I guess I'm sort of in love with him, too. But I saw. I saw his face in the clearing when he thought you were dead. And I heard the way he said your name. And then . . . I knew, you know? The two of you were meant to be. So I'm sure."

"A leopard?" Galen's mother said, shaking out her topaz-colored hair. "Why, dear, that's wonderful. Your great-great-grandmother was a leopard."

"You gave up being a bird for me," Keller whispered in his ear.

"I think I could learn to like running," he murmured, and took the chance to touch his lips to her cheek.

• • •

"No, ma'am, I'm really sorry I woke you up," Keller said. "Yes, ma'am, I do know how late it is." She strained to hear the voice on the other end of the phone. She had a finger in her ear to try and block out the noise of the wild celebration around her, but it wasn't doing much good.

"Because I honestly don't think it's funny," Iliana's mother said. "The baby is just fine; he's been in his bed all night. Why would you think he wasn't?"

"Well, ma'am, it's hard to explain . . ."

"And now he's awake, and he's going to start crying—well, he's not crying. But now he wants to eat the phone . . . Alex!"

A voice on the other end squealed and said distinctly, "Kee-kee!"

"Yeah, it's Kee-kee," Keller said, startled. "Um, I'm glad you're okay, kid. And, see, I didn't go bye-bye after all. So you may think you're pretty smart, but you still have something to learn about precognition, hotshot. Right?" Keller added, "You know I thought for a minute once that you might be the Wild Power. But I guess you're just a good old-fashioned witch baby."

Iliana, who was passing by, gave her a very strange look. "Keller, are you having a conversation with my baby brother?"

"What *exactly* did the dragon say?" Mother Cybele asked anxiously. Although she looked like a big dove and her eyes were always kind, there was a firmness about her plump chin that Keller liked.

"I asked who woke him up. And he said"—Keller reached for the exact words—"he said, 'Someone you'll never know. A witch who isn't a witch. We made our own alliance.'"

"A witch who isn't a witch," Mother Cybele repeated.

Aradia's face was sober. "I wonder who that could be. And where they are now."

Mother Cybele said quietly, "Time will tell."

"The police are already inside," Nissa said, holding the cell phone to her ear as she talked to Keller. "I guess the kids at the party called them when they saw a panther. They've found the family . . . Mr. and Ms. Ashton-Hughes and Jaime and Brett. They're taking them to the hospital."

She snapped the phone shut. "We'd better send some witches to the hospital. But as long as they're alive, they have a pretty good chance, don't you think? After all, we've got a Wild Power with healing fire. Now, can't you relax and try to enjoy yourself?"

It was two days later. Keller was sitting in a sunny alcove in the safe house where Iliana and Galen and the others had been brought to protect them from the Night World. And to give them a chance to recover.

It was nice to be still for a while. To sit and read . . . and think. And it was even nicer to be able to do it with Galen around.

He came in the door quietly—he always moved cat-quietly now. She smiled at him. He looked so wonderfully dear with his golden hair and fairy-tale looks and leopard-green eyes.

"I wrote you a poem," he said, sitting down beside her. "Well, no, that's not true. I kind of stole what your mother wrote and made it into . . . something. I don't know what. But I think maybe it's what she really meant to say, after all."

Keller blinked at him, then looked down at the piece of paper he gave her.

People die . . . so love them every day.
Beauty fades . . . so look before it's gone.
Love changes . . . but not the love you give.
And if you love, you'll never be alone.

"Actually, I was going to say, 'And you will always be alone . . . so don't rely on others for your happiness, but don't stop loving, either, because then you'll end up empty and alone instead of alone and strong and able to give without worrying about what you're going to get back.' But that was kind of long, and it didn't scan," he said.

Keller stared down at the paper blindly.

"I'm sorry," he said. "If you don't like it—"

Keller threw her arms around him, and her tears spilled over. "I'm going to burn the other one," she said. "And I love you. Kiss me."

He grinned. "Yes, Boss."

And he did.

One from the land of kings long forgotten;
One from the hearth which still holds the spark;
One from the Day World where two eyes are watching;
One from the twilight to be one with the dark.

See where it all began
in *Night World*,
by L. J. Smith.

It was on the first day of summer vacation that Poppy found out she was going to die.

It happened on Monday, the first *real* day of vacation (the weekend didn't count). Poppy woke up feeling gloriously weightless and thought, *No school.* Sunlight was streaming in the window, turning the sheer hangings around her bed filmy gold. Poppy pushed them aside and jumped out of bed—and winced.

Ouch. That pain in her stomach again. Sort of a gnawing, as if something were eating its way toward her back. It helped a little if she bent over.

No, Poppy thought. I refuse to be sick during summer vacation. I *refuse.* A little power of positive thinking is what's needed here.

Grimly, doubled over—think positive, idiot!—she made her way down the hall to the turquoise-and-gold-tiled bathroom.

At first she thought she was going to throw up, but then the pain eased as suddenly as it had come. Poppy straightened and regarded her tousled reflection triumphantly.

"Stick with me, kid, and you'll be fine," she whispered to it, and gave a conspiratorial wink. Then she leaned forward, seeing her own green eyes narrow in suspicion. There on her nose were four freckles. Four and a half, if she were completely honest, which Poppy North usually was. How childish, how—*cute!* Poppy stuck her tongue out at herself and then turned away with great dignity, without bothering to comb the wild coppery curls that clustered over her head.

She maintained the dignity until she got to the kitchen, where Phillip, her twin brother, was eating Special K. Then she narrowed her eyes again, this time at him. It was bad enough to be small, slight, and curly-haired—to look, in fact, as much like an elf as anything she'd ever seen sitting on a buttercup in a children's picture book—but to have a twin who was tall, Viking-blond, and classically handsome . . . well, that just showed a certain deliberate malice in the makeup of the universe, didn't it?

"Hello, Phillip," she said in a voice heavy with menace.

Phillip, who was used to his sister's moods, was unimpressed. He lifted his gaze from the comic section of the *L.A. Times* for a moment. Poppy had to admit that he had nice eyes: questing green eyes with very dark lashes. They were the only thing the twins had in common.

"Hi," Phillip said flatly, and went back to the comics. Not many kids Poppy knew read the newspaper, but that was Phil all over. Like Poppy, he'd been a junior at El Camino High last year, and unlike Poppy, he'd made straight As while starring on the football team, the hockey team, and the baseball team. Also serving as class president. One of Poppy's greatest joys in life was teasing him. She thought he was too straitlaced.

Just now she giggled and shrugged, giving up the menacing look. "Where's Cliff and Mom?" Cliff Hilgard was their stepfather of three years and even straighter-laced than Phil.

"Cliff's at work. Mom's getting dressed. You'd better eat something or she'll get on your case."

"Yeah, yeah . . ." Poppy went on tiptoe to rummage through a cupboard. Finding a box of Frosted Flakes, she thrust a hand in and delicately pulled out one flake. She ate it dry.

It wasn't *all* bad being short and elfin. She did a few dance steps to the refrigerator, shaking the cereal box in rhythm.

"I'm a . . . sex pixie!" she sang, giving it a foot-stomping rhythm.

"No, you're not," Phillip said with devastating calm. "And why don't you put some clothes on?"

Holding the refrigerator door open, Poppy looked down at herself. She was wearing the oversize T-shirt she'd slept in. It covered her like a minidress. "This *is* clothes," she said serenely, taking a Diet Coke from the fridge.

There was a knock at the kitchen door. Poppy saw who it was through the screen.

"Hi, James! C'mon in."

James Rasmussen came in, taking off his wraparound Ray-Bans. Looking at him, Poppy felt a pang—as always. It didn't matter that she had seen him every day, practically, for the past ten years. She still felt a quick sharp throb in her chest, somewhere between sweetness and pain, when first confronted with him every morning.

It wasn't just his outlaw good looks, which always reminded her vaguely of James Dean. He had silky light brown hair, a subtle, intelligent face, and gray eyes that were alternately intense and cool. He was the handsomest boy at El Camino High, but that wasn't it, that wasn't what Poppy responded to. It was something *inside* him, something mysterious and compelling and always just out of reach. It made her heart beat fast and her skin tingle.

Phillip felt differently. As soon as James came in, he stiffened and his face went cold. Electric dislike flashed between the two boys.

Then James smiled faintly, as if Phillip's reaction amused him. "Hi."

"Hi," Phil said, not thawing in the least. Poppy had the strong sense that he'd like to bundle her up and rush her out of the room. Phillip always overdid the protective-brother bit when James was around. "So how's Jacklyn and Michaela?" he added nastily.

James considered. "Well, I don't really know."

"You don't *know*? Oh, yeah, you always drop your girlfriends just before summer vacation. Leaves you free to maneuver, right?"

"Of course," James said blandly. He smiled.

Phillip glared at him with unabashed hatred.

Poppy, for her part, was seized by joy. Goodbye, Jacklyn; goodbye Michaela. Goodbye to Jacklyn's elegant long legs and Michaela's amazing pneumatic chest. This was going to be a wonderful summer.

Many people thought Poppy and James's relationship platonic. This wasn't true. Poppy had known for years that she was going to marry him. It was one of her two great ambitions, the other being to see the world. She just hadn't gotten around to informing James yet. Right now he still thought he liked long-legged girls with salon fingernails and Italian pumps.

"Is that a new CD?" she said, to distract him from his stare out with his future brother-in-law.

James hefted it. "It's the new Ethnotechno release."

Poppy cheered. "More Tuva throat singers—I can't *wait*. Let's go listen to it." But just then her mother walked in. Poppy's mother was cool, blond, and perfect, like an Alfred Hitchcock heroine. She normally wore an expression of effortless efficiency. Poppy, heading out of the kitchen, nearly ran into her.

"Sorry—morning!"

"Hold on a minute," Poppy's mother said, getting hold of Poppy by the back of her T-shirt. "Good morning, Phil; good morning, James," she added. Phil said good morning and James nodded, ironically polite.

"Has everybody had breakfast?" Poppy's mother asked, and when the boys said they had, she looked at her daughter. "And what about you?" she asked, gazing into Poppy's face.

Poppy rattled the Frosted Flakes box and her mother winced. "Why don't you at least put milk on them?"

"Better this way," Poppy said firmly, but when her mother gave her a little push toward the refrigerator, she went and got a quart carton of lowfat milk.

"What are you planning to do with your first day of freedom?" her mother said, glancing from James to Poppy.

"Oh, I don't know." Poppy looked at James. "Listen to some music; maybe go up to the hills? Or drive to the beach?"

"Whatever you want," James said. "We've got all summer."

The summer stretched out in front of Poppy, hot and golden and resplendent. It smelled like pool chlorine and sea salt; it felt like warm grass under her back. Three whole months, she thought. That's forever. Three months is forever.

It was strange that she was actually thinking this when it happened.

"We could check out the new shops at the Village—" she

was beginning, when suddenly the pain struck and her breath caught in her throat.

It was bad—a deep, twisting burst of agony that made her double over. The milk carton flew from her fingers and everything went gray.